THE FAMILY OF WILLIAM NEILSON BOOK II

A CHALICE ARGENT

James Buchan

MLP

Copyright © 2023 James Buchan

The right of James Buchan to be identified as the Author of the Work has been asserted by him in accordance with the Copyright, Designs and Patents Act 1988.

Illustration & Map by Emily Faccini

First published in Great Britain in 2023 by
Mountain Leopard Press
An imprint of Welbeck Publishing Group

First published as a paperback in Great Britain in 2025 by
Mountain Leopard Press
An imprint of Headline Publishing Group Limited

1

Apart from any use permitted under UK copyright law, this publication may only be reproduced, stored, or transmitted, in any form, or by any means, with prior permission in writing of the publishers or, in the case of reprographic production, in accordance with the terms of licences issued by the Copyright Licensing Agency.

All characters in this publication are fictitious and any resemblance to real persons, living or dead, is purely coincidental.

Cataloguing in Publication Data is available from the British Library

PB ISBN 978 1 80069 903 8

Typeset in Adobe Cason
Printed and bound in Great Britain by Clays Ltd, Elcograf S.p.A.

Headline's policy is to use papers that are natural, renewable and recyclable products and made from wood grown in well-managed forests and other controlled sources. The logging and manufacturing processes are expected to conform to the environmental regulations of the country of origin.

HEADLINE PUBLISHING GROUP
An Hachette UK Company
Carmelite House
50 Victoria Embankment
London EC4Y 0DZ

The authorised representative in the EEA is
Hachette Ireland, 8 Castlecourt Centre,
Dublin 15, D15 XTP3, Ireland
(email: info@hbgi.ie)

www.headline.co.uk
www.hachette.co.uk

JAMES BUCHAN is a novelist and historian, whose books have won many prizes and been translated into a dozen foreign languages. He has written widely on the modern history of Scotland, most recently in *John Law: A Scottish Adventurer of the Eighteenth Century*. He is a fellow of the Royal Society of Literature. He lives on a farm in Norfolk.

Praise for James Buchan

"An epic voyage well worth taking ... exhilarating"
MARIANKA SWAIN, *Telegraph*

"I don't believe this country has a better writer to offer than James Buchan"
MICHAEL HOFMANN, *London Review of Books*

"There is nothing quite like a James Buchan novel"
JOHN SELF, *Financial Times*

"One of our finest writers"   JOHN BURNSIDE, *The Times*

"A hugely readable adventure-romance encompassing imperial France, the East India Company, Persia, the Jacobite rebellion, shipwreck, duels, derring-do and more. Buchan ... really knows how to construct a ripping tale"
ADAM ROBERTS, *Guardian*

ALSO BY JAMES BUCHAN

FICTION

A Parish of Rich Women

Davy Chadwick

Slide

Heart's Journey in Winter

High Latitudes: A Romance

A Good Place to Die

The Gate of Air

A Street Shaken by Light,
The Family of William Neilson Book I

NON-FICTION

Jeddah: Old and New

Frozen Desire: An Enquiry into the Meaning of Money

Capital of the Mind: How Edinburgh Changed the World

Adam Smith and the Pursuit of Perfect Liberty

Days of God: The Revolution in Iran and Its Consequences

John Law: A Scottish Adventurer of the Eighteenth Century

CONTENTS

PART 1 9
The Foundling

PART 2 157
Under the Leads

PART 3 209
A Dusty Bridegroom

Il faut de plus grandes vertus pour soutenir la bonne fortune que la mauvaise

Happiness demands more of the character than does misfortune

Duc de La Rochefoucauld

PART I

A Foundling

I

In the Kingdom of France and of Navarre, between the Loire river and its tributary, the Cher, there is a district known as La Sologne. It is a poor country of sand and heather, few or no villages, wide skies and innumerable ponds and meres.

The principal house in the Sologne is named La Ferté-Joyeuse. It stands on the left bank of a stream called the Sauldre. Once a strong place of the counts of Joyeuse, that held for twelve days and nights against Prince Edward of Wales and Aquitaine, La Ferté-Joyeuse had in the intervening ages gained in extent and amenity, as had the whole kingdom. The erection of the Joyeuse county into a dukedom, in the reign of François I, brought to the wicked donjon brick towers at the four corners a forest of slate rooves and an iron lantern, the which added to the beauty of the castle without repairing its inconveniency. Set into the brick walls were tablets and quoins of Normandie stone so that all should know that it was not from parsimony that the dukes of Joyeuse built in brick.

Had any poor man or woman been abroad this night of Saint-Silvestre, December 31, 1746, with rain falling in curtains and chimney-smoke rolling earthward off the eaves; or, better, some storm-cock beating through the streaming air to find a temporarie rest on a flag-staff, this would have been the terrestrial view. Before the portal of the house, on an esplanade bounded by a trench or moat, low pavilions served one to shelter the corps of guard and the other the kitchens and bake-house. Beyond a ramped bridge over the moat, two ranges, called commons, each of which had kept a regiment dry during the Fronde, slid away into deluge.

The western or right-hand range was appropriated to a tennis-court, fencing-school, manedge and other hygienic or martial offices. Behind it was the mains or home farm. In the left-hand or eastern of the commons, which housed the stables, smiddy, fabricks and suchlike policies, in the hay-loft above the coach-house, Nicole or Nicolette Marrin, lady's maid, and Pierre Dalouhe, under-groom, are doing what young persons love to do. The youth stops and listens.

"Ah Pierrot, were you not happy like so?"

"I heard an evil sound. Don't move an inch, duckling."

The moment passes. Mme Nicolette rises, adjusts her skirts, lights a lantern. In the door-way on the court, her friend is standing in his sodden shirt.

"What is it, Pierre?"

"A dying horse. A dead gentleman."

In the economy of their love, Pierre Dalouhe has but to be the dearest thing that ever walked the ground of France. On Mme Nicolette fall the duties of reflection and decision. She holds the light over the fallen man. She bends down, touches his cold lips. She opens his coat and sees, across his tunic, a dirty blue ribbon. She parts his shirt and places her hand on his heart. In the lantern-light, she finds against the man's chest, sewn into his shirt, a square of linen, and the remnant of an embroidered crown and cap and an obliterated blazon. About his boots the water in the lantern-light is red with blood. Mme Nicolette straightens.

"Cut his boots off, boy. Stop, if you can, the bleeding. Then come to the back door to hear Her Ladyship's orders." Mme Nicolette hitches up her skirt-hems and splashes through sheets of water towards the bridge.

The castellane must have expressed an inclination, for a little later Pierre Dalouhe is carrying the man on his shoulder to a small room in the south-eastern tower that overlooks the kitchen range. There, while Mme Nicolette makes up a bed, M. Pierre cuts up horse-bandages for the patient's ankles. Their work will have proceeded with greater despatch except for bumps, slaps, pinches, trips, pokes, tickles, nuzzles, touches and kisses such as occur between persons who still have love's business to transact. At length, the man is settled in his cot. Pierre Dalouhe is riffling through his saddle-bags. In a document case, he finds, and presents to his darling, a sealed packet.

Mme Nicolette, no more than any other confidential servant, is no respecter of seals. With her friend holding a candle, and with the care of one who has but lately mastered the art, she reads the magnificent document.

"What does it say, Nicou?" M. Dalouhe is eager to move to the succeeding item of agenda.

"Never you mind. I am taking it to Her Ladyship. By God, Pierre Dalouhe, if you breathe one word of this letter to the wind, you will say farewell to your little playmate in my skirts."

II

I dreamed I was in Drumelzier church and François Delacour was standing beside me. In a body, the Kirk Session inspected M. Delacour, and then me, and processed to their places. I saw the *Prince-de-Conty* breaking and Father Patrick in the howling foam, rising and falling. I saw the flash of the mine at the gate of Gingie Fort. The Irish men I killed on Culloden Moor stared at me in rebuke.

Standing mute before was a veiled woman who would be my conductress into the dark. I sat up and said:

"I have seen the limits of the earth and found nothing worthy of report."

She turned away from me and disappeared.

I dreamed I was dreaming, and woke.

III

I opened my eyes. In the window-light, a small girl was waxing boots. She was a skinny little thing, with black fingers and a smudged face, and a second-hand dress and apron. She had no cap. She looked at me and started.

I tried to smile at her.

She said: "I may not speak to you or I will be punished."

"I would not wish that, young mistress. Do not speak."

I lay on my side and watched her work. She placed the waxed boots in the basket, and took out the next pair. She might have been pretty, had she less work to do and more food to eat.

She said: "I am the lowest servant in the house and won't understand a word of your heathen babble. Anyway, you will be dead by evening."

It seemed the lass was of so small account that people spoke in front of her as if she were a stool or pail. I understood that she was a sort of process-verbal of every conversation in the house.

"I do not intend to die, miss."

The girl stole a glance at me lest, by my flagrant contradiction, I, too, would be punished. Then, in a rush:

"I am glad, sir."

"Now, do not speak, young miss. I shall watch you work, if I may."

She became conscious of herself, polished the boots to a sheen that flashed the window-light, tossed the completed pair into the basket with a fantastical disinvolture.

"Sir?"

I put up my hand to cover my mouth. The lass began to fidget. I feared she might burst.

"Speak, miss."

"Did you ever once see Her Ladyship?"

"I did see her, miss. Many years ago, in another country."

"I would so very much like to see Her Ladyship."

"She is beautiful and kind. Now I must sleep, miss, for I do not wish to die."

I dozed to the slap of brushes.

"Sir?"

"Yes, miss?"

"I did not tell the truth. It was Christmas Day in the morning. I was skinning rabbits at the kitchen door. There was frost on the stones. Her Ladyship was mounting the coach. Madame Nicole was with her and shouted at me to go in-doors."

"Do not take it ill, miss."

"No, sir."

She laid down her brushes.

"Sir?"

"Yes, miss?"

"If Her Ladyship is beautiful, why does she wear a veil?"

IV

In my dreaming, I was standing in the shareholders' gallery of Mr Law's bank at Paris. All about were wooden scaffolds spattered with paint and lime. Above my head were clouds and heroes and goddesses, some painted, some but scratches in the wet plaster. A young lady was stepping away from me through the rubbish. She was in Court dress, her long hair piled up on her head and looped with pearls. Somebody was calling her from the depths of the gallery, but the girl did not mend her step. I said: "At the end, mademoiselle, do not turn your head. Whatever you do, mademoiselle, do not turn your head."

The young lady stopped; and then, to cross me, she turned her face on me and I woke.

"Miss?"

"Yes, sir?"

"Come close."

"I am frightened, sir."

"Do not be. This pocket. If I die. Give it to Her Ladyship. For King James."

"How will I see Her Ladyship?"

"In the night. Kneel by her bed. Call her name quietly. Do not touch Her Ladyship."

"For King John."
"King James. At night. Do not touch Her Ladyship."
"I would so very much like to touch Her Ladyship."
"Do not touch Her Ladyship."
"I am frightened, sir."
"Do not be. I am with you always. Do not touch Her Ladyship."
"Do not touch Her Ladyship."

V

I remembered the battle in Scotland and fought it every hour to defeat. Of what happened after, how my life was saved, and how I came to be in France, and at my lady's country-house, I had no recollection. In a half-dream, I thought to hear kittiwakes, in tens of thousands. I brought all my mental force to bear on the sound, but nothing came of it. I had crossed some Lethe of forgetting. I remembered nothing until I saw the servant girl putting wax on boots.

"Madame?"
"He speaks! And in godly French!"
"Madame…?"

"Nicolette."

"Madame Nicolette, what are they saying of me in the house?"

"Five-to-one to live. Eighties to marry Mme la marquise. Both lengthened from last week."

"I suggest that you take the fives, madame."

"I have taken the eighties. Remember that, if you live, Mister the Colonel Neilson, Scottish gentleman, knight of the royal and military order of Saint-Louis, travelling into Italy on the King's particular business."

VI

Mme Nicolette held in two hands a jug of liquid. The scent of it made me swoon. With infinite care, she held it out to me.

"Is that milk?"

"Milk! It is Mouron's milk, sweeter than honey, richer than Brittany butter. There is no finer in France."

"Who, if I may inquire, is Mouron?"

"You have not heard of Mouron? Thirteen milkings and still the queen of the herd? Whom M. le duc d'Estampes tried to steal for one thousand crowns but Her Ladyship would not agree?"

I took the smallest sop.

"Admirable, Mme Nicolette."

She looked away into old recollections. "I was her milker. No other girl could approach her."

I found it hard to convert Mme Nicolette into a milk-maid.

"But no longer?"

She turned back to me. "I became ill and Her Ladyship nursed me and, when I was myself again, brought me in-doors to be beside her at all times."

"Ah."

"And what does 'ah' mean, Mr Colonel?"

"Nothing whatever. It is a Scottish way of speech."

Mme Nicolette was not satisfied, but had something to say of greater importance.

"Her Ladyship is sending you this very morning her personal physician."

"Dear Mme Nicolette, will you do me the greatest kindness? Would you ask M. Dalouhe to clean and charge my pistols and place them in my reach on the night-table? When the learned gentleman comes to call, as soon as you admit him, you will oblige me if you will walk to that corner, turn your back and cover your face with your hands. The room is small and I would not wish my friend to suffer a powder burn."

"Her Ladyship will not be pleased."

"I must take that at risk."

The quacker did not keep his engagement. A quarter-hour later, Mme Nicolette brought me a letter which read:

"Mme de Maurepas finds that if Colonel Neilson is well enough to assassinate her physician, he is well enough to depart La Ferté-Joyeuse and continue his journey into Italy. She regrets that she is not able in person to bid him Godspeed. She has left with her maidservant letters to the postmasters at Vierzon and Bourges, and to Messrs the Aldermen of Marseille."

"Mme Nicolette, will you do me the favour of having me brought a razor and some water? I am to wait on Mme de Maurepas."

"She shall not receive you, Colonel."

"Tens says Her Ladyship will receive me."

"I have no relish today for wagers."

We had reached the door in the wall. I unlocked and opened it.

"Mme Nicolette, I know what ails your mistress and I know also the remedy. Also, on another matter, I would be obliged to you if you would return to me a hand-kerchief that I had with me on my arrival and that I rather value."

Mme Nicolette sulked.

"Worn out as it is, it shows a silver cup on a black field or, as the heralds say: 'Sable, ane cover'd chalice argent'."

Mme Nicolette said nothing.

I said: "At the base of the turnpike stair is what?"

"Map room."

"Next?"

"My lady's laboratory."

"Then?"

"Duke's first withdrawing room. Picture gallery. My lady's cabinet. First antichamber. Second antichamber. Oratory. Bedchamber."

"Menservants?"

"Four guards in the second antichamber."

"Will Mme Nicolette have the goodness to detain them?"

"How?"

"How the hell do I know? I am not a woman."

At length, Mme Nicolette said: "If you injure my mistress, Mr Colonel, I shall cut off your ugly Scottish balls and stuff them down your throat."

"I would expect no less from a good servant, Mme Nicolette."

"Two raps on the outer door. Count one-two-three. Two more raps."

"Of course."

VII

For the remainder of the day, I experimented walking. My boots were not to be found so I toddled in my stockings, which had the virtue of making no sound. As the light diminished, a mist came down on the house like a drenched cloak, and seemed to penetrate in-doors. A clock from the commons called out the quarters, and the halves and the hours. It grew dark. The sounds of the house and the kitchen, made indistinct by the fog, abated. Taking up my night-light, I paddled to the turnpike stair.

The rooms below passed in a fever. Presses, tables, globes, glass vessels, furnaces approached in the lamp-light and receded. I came into a gallery hanging with portrait pictures. I raised my light and saw duke after duke after count after count of Joyeuse, extending in line unbroken to the Flood. I limped to a canapé to rest my legs and regarded one of the Joyeuse paragons. He wore, above spotless linen and lace, the skin of some wild animal and leaned at ease upon an oaken club. I could hear, muffled, the sounds of men's voices and women's laughter. I passed through two more chambers, then a little shrine with lights on the altar, and found myself before the famous door. I knocked twice, paused, then knocked twice more, and turned the handle.

The curtains were drawn together, and the only light came from the dancing flames of the hearth-fire. A woman sat upright in a wing-chair. Though she was veiled, something in her shape or posture was known to me. She turned her veiled face at me.

"Will Mme de Maurepas do me the honour of lifting her veil?"

The lady stood up. "I did not ask you to come to my house, Colonel Neilson. I have had my people tend you, for the love of God, but now I wish you to leave. If you stay here one instant more, I shall call my servants."

"Mme la marquise de Maurepas, do you think that I will be scared away, I who got off that bloody moor . . ."

Mme de Maurepas fell a-tremble. "I heard you did great honour to yourself . . ."

". . . that I shall be scared away by a pimple on my mistress' cheek?"

"You, too, know nothing. Go to Italy with my blessing,

which I believe is the most sincere you will ever have received."

"Show me your face, Mme de Maurepas."

Mme la marquise de Maurepas took a step forward. "Look at me, Mr Neilson, if you can. Let me see what the hero of Culloden Moor is made of."

She took the hem of her veil in both hands. She said: "Look at me, Mr Neilson."

She lifted up her bare face in the fire-light. Nothing in my life had prepared me for such a sight.

I said: "Will she permit me to kiss the face that I have loved so many years?"

"No."

"Will she permit me to touch her neck or breast?"

"No."

"In one or two days, Mme la marquise will lose her eye-sight. Will she oblige me by calling her maidservant?"

Mme de Maurepas pointed to a bell-cord by the chimney. She let fall the veil. I rang and Mme Nicolette, who seemed to have been not far away, rapped and entered.

Mme la marquise said: "What requests Colonel Neilson now makes of you or any of my people, I would wish to be carried out to the letter."

VIII

I was down in the dark before the house and found my way, blind and guideless, to the dairy. Nothing had been done to my satisfaction. On the stone floor, there were splinters of wood staves where a servant had smashed a barrel of vinegar and thought his work fairly done. I sensed I was not a favourite in the mains. In one of the milking-stalls there was tether'd a brindled cow, bellowing, without a stick of hay to eat, and neither brushed nor washed. Her udder was tight as a kettle-drum. I shook down some hay for her and woke the kitchen for two pails of hot water. Neither I nor the beast were in especially good moods.

"Now, Mistress Mouron," I said, drawing up my stool. "We can do this pleasantly and expeditiously or we can fight. It is your choice."

A hoof sent the bucket flying against the long wall and me across the floor. From that elevation, I saw the ladies enter. "She won't let him near, my lady. I told you so."

I picked myself up. Mme de Maurepas wore, over her dress, a shift of coarse fustian cloth, her hair confined to the last strand in a cap of the same stuff. She had patens over her slippers. She was veiled. Mme Nicolette, dressed alike sans veil, looked at me in contempt.

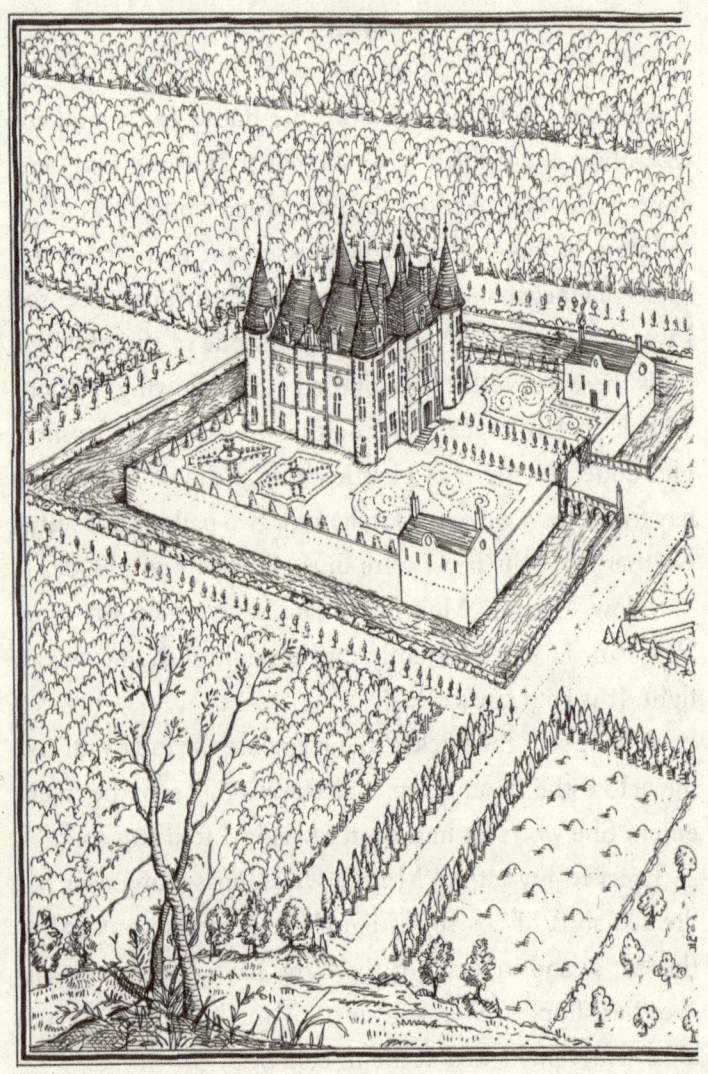

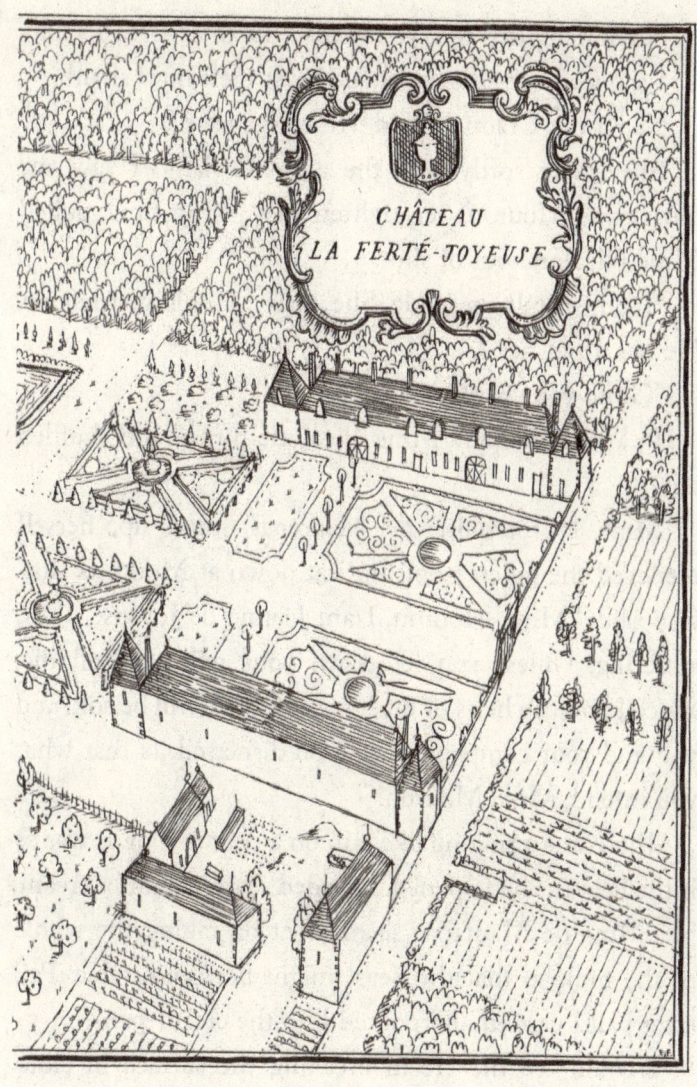

"I am delighted to give my place to an expert," I said.

I sconced myself against the beast's left hind shank.

"Go away, Colonel," said Mme Nicolette.

She spoke softly into the animal's flank. I saw the muscles of Mouron's leg tighten and, just in time, pulled Mme Nicolette out of shot.

"It's his fault, my lady. She does not allow strangers. He has upset her."

"Go to your work, Marrin."

In a sort of agony, Mme Nicolette turned and shuffled out.

Mme la marquise de Maurepas stood up, herself retrieved the fallen stool, and sat down at Mouron's side. She said: "Mme Mouron, I am Jeanne de Joyeuse. I am suffering. Unless you let down your milk, I shall die. Since I have no heirs of my body, my lands will be sold and you and your companions will be dispersed. Is that what you intend, Mme Mouron?"

There was a ringing like rain on a church roof. It was as if the heavens had opened. I needed scarce a pint of cream, but Mme de Maurepas seemed set on taking the whole of the milk so that the beast might be comfortable. Pail after pail I carried and poured into the cream-pans.

I could see the cream breaking the surface in clots.

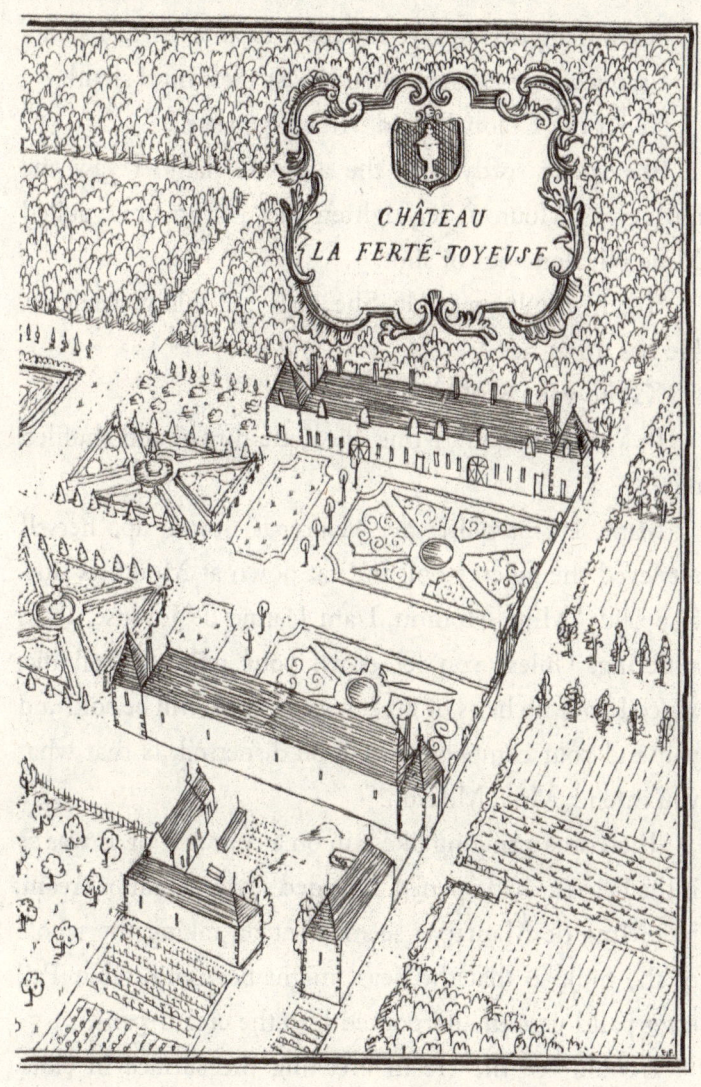

"I am delighted to give my place to an expert," I said.

I sconced myself against the beast's left hind shank.

"Go away, Colonel," said Mme Nicolette.

She spoke softly into the animal's flank. I saw the muscles of Mouron's leg tighten and, just in time, pulled Mme Nicolette out of shot.

"It's his fault, my lady. She does not allow strangers. He has upset her."

"Go to your work, Marrin."

In a sort of agony, Mme Nicolette turned and shuffled out.

Mme la marquise de Maurepas stood up, herself retrieved the fallen stool, and sat down at Mouron's side. She said: "Mme Mouron, I am Jeanne de Joyeuse. I am suffering. Unless you let down your milk, I shall die. Since I have no heirs of my body, my lands will be sold and you and your companions will be dispersed. Is that what you intend, Mme Mouron?"

There was a ringing like rain on a church roof. It was as if the heavens had opened. I needed scarce a pint of cream, but Mme de Maurepas seemed set on taking the whole of the milk so that the beast might be comfortable. Pail after pail I carried and poured into the cream-pans.

I could see the cream breaking the surface in clots.

I stood idle in the cold light, Mouron champed and wheezed while Mme de Maurepas dozed in the heat from the brindled pelt. A pair of cats rubbed against her skirts, eager to assist. Sparrows chattled in the eaves. Every while and then, I skimmed off some of the cream to experiment.

After an half-hour, I said: "Will you kindly stand before me and lift your veil?"

As a child, in the summers in the Scottish Borders, I used to watch my grandmother making pultises to treat the hands when they fell sick or injured. In her style, I made a sort of cake of Mouron's cream and rubbed it over my lady's whole face and neck down to the bosom. Mme de Maurepas flinched, not with pain, but at the insult to her modesty. I was falling into reverie.

Mme de Maurepas stepped back and said: "καὶ ἀφροδισίων ἔργων ἐπί τε γυναικείων σωμάτων καὶ ἀνδρῴων, ἐλευθέρων τε καὶ δούλων."

My Greek was not what it once was, but I recognised the Oath of Hippocrates. The physician should in no wise take amorous advantage of the patient, lass or lad, free or enslaved.

"Is that the case?"

I scraped the cream and blisters into a basin. With

my back to Mme de Maurepas, I covered the basin with mousseline and placed it on a high shelf.

"Will she do me the kindness to meet me here at precisely the same time next morning?"

"No. Her maid-servant shall conduct the treatment."

Damn!

"As you command, my lady."

"Kindly, leave me and send Marrin to me."

As she turned away, I reached for my basin and placed it under my coat.

Outside, poor Mme Nicolette was in tears. Her cheeks and dress were spattered with shite. At the end of the byre, broken up by bars of dawn sunlight, was a force of men and girls, in a fine mood. Mme Nicolette slid past me into the milking-hall.

I walked towards the milkers. As I approached, there was a shuffling back and forward among the girls, and a wiping of hands on skirts.

"Now, my fine people. I have excellent news for you. Contrary to all that you have been told, Mme la marquise de Maurepas is not going to die but she is going to live. She will, as she recovers, wish to know who of her servants had stood true to her in her illness, and who had sold her butter and cream for their private advantage."

I did not know if that was true, but it did not have to be true.

I turned my back on them and continued my promenade.

I said: "You do not have to work for Mme de Maurepas. There are good farms in this great land of France, though perhaps not in this district, that would be happy to take men and girls dismissed for stealing from Mme la marquise de Maurepas."

I turned again. They did not look so brave.

"Now, all of you, to the pump! Now! And wash your shitty hands before you dare to touch Her Ladyship's animals."

The girls slithered past me.

"And you, M. Jean!"

A man, square as a mason's shed, stiffened but stood his ground.

"You are not chief stockman for nothing, M. Jean. Control your people, or I shall do it for you."

IX

I did not especially resent being excluded from the surgery. I misliked death by famine. I had not eaten at all in the days of my convalessing, and my sally that morning into the open air had made me hungry as a dog. By the middle of the night, with not so much as a cup of whey to keep me clagged to earth, I resolved that Mme la marquise de Maurepas and her Mme Nicolette were occupied with physick, and that I must forage for myself. I descended to the map-room, where the candle-light flickered among the globes on a dead body. As I stumbled to it, it sat up. It was the little kitchen-maid. She sprang to her feet.

"What are you doing in the dark, sir?"

"I am hungry. What are you doing, miss?"

"I am frightened."

"Weel, shall we not unite our forces and deploy our peculiar strengths? You shall show me to the panetrie, and I shall guard you while you sleep."

"The store cupboards are locked."

"Are there not some rests? The end of a rib of beef or a couple of river-trout that were too much of a good thing? Or half a venison pastie more suited as midday fare? Or perhaps a damson-tart that Her Ladyship found sharp?"

"There's a bin where the cooks put the uneaten bread for crumbs."

"Excellent. You shall reveal me the pantrie, where I shall riot on stale bread. Then we shall find you a cosie place to sleep and I shall fetch my pistols and sit a little way off."

We made our way to a stair-case. The door at its head opened, and Mme Nicolette tip-taed through, her slippers in her hand. We looked at each and one another.

Mme Nicolette was the first to recover. "What are you doing here, orphan-girl? You are not permitted to leave the dormitory. I shall tell Her Ladyship and she will send you back to the Hospital."

"I shall kill myself first."

"Please, dear Mme Nicolette, can you not tell that they are bullying her? See how her dress is torn and her face is scratched."

"That, Mr Colonel, is the life of the underservant. I knew that life. And now, sir, may I ask you why you train about Her Ladyship's house at midnight like an unhappy burglar?"

"I am hungry. I had not breakfast, dinner nor supper."

"Virgin! Her Ladyship gave precise orders for your entertainment."

"We're damned if we'll wait on a heretic and a sponger."

"You rascal! How dare you speak of Her Ladyship's guest in that way!"

"Mme Nicolette, the lass repeats what she hears."

"Chalice! Her Ladyship will turn them all out and good riddance."

She thought for a moment.

"Come with me, girl. And you, Colonel, are you able to make your own way to your room? I do not wish to add to the cares of my mistress. I shall not report this incident to Her Ladyship."

Who might inquire in turn what you were doing in the dark with your shoes in your hands and hay in your hair and a smile like a petted angel.

"Still on eighties, Mme Nicolette?"

"Eighties? Pouf! I can lay thirty-threes at best."

I was drawing breath at my chamber-table when the door opened, and the kitchen-maid slid in behind a trey. On it was a candle, which showed a whole cold fowl, salad, sweet things and a bottle of white Burgundy wine. I suppose it was put out each night in the mistaken belief that Mme de Maurepas was subject to hunger. The girl's scratches had been washed. She scented of vinegar.

"What a feast we shall have this midnight, young miss!

Now you sit down on the bed and spread this napeking to protect your dress, and I shall carve Madame In-Case. Will you take white meat, from the breast-bone, or the darker flesh from the leg?"

"White. No. Dark. No. White."

"I shall carve you both, and show you how we soldiers dine on the march. Watch! We take a tranche of bread and, when as now we have it, spread it with butter. We place on it the flesh, and a very little pinch of salt, and then some green stuff, so. Then we close it with a second tranche of bread. There! Take it! You have your dinner in one hand."

"Mew won burr logship clurch og nach day, shir?"

"Forgive me, miss. The universal fault of veteran soldiers is deafness. It is the consequence of the combustive ordnance deployed on the modern battlefield. In contrast, as you know, the pitched battles of antiquity were silent affairs."

"Plunk bong lerderrsherp swet chicken easy day, slir?"

"I think she does, miss, but not at every repast. Else, she might tire of it."

"How could anybody tlur of chodkin?"

"I am sure I don't know. Now, young madame, will you join me in a glass of wine?"

"Yer never tested wine."

"Then I shall pour you a small glass, and myself glug from the bottle. Wait! If I am not mistaken, the sillabob is made of the famous sweet wine of Sauternes. That shall be your ration of the grape, while I shall do very well with the pear. Since we have become such friends, young miss, will you not tell me your name?"

There was no answer. I turned. The child was asleep. I drank my wine, ate the pear that must have lain all winter in the ice-house, laid over the kitchen-maid my cloak and left the room, leaving the sillabob for her breakfast and the door open. Curled up in a window-bay, I counted my blessings. The shorter odds or, as we say, tighter market on matrimony could arise only in some progress in Mme de Maurepas's recovery. I blessed the Providence that had once taken me to Isfahan in Persia, and kept me idle there in the cool season.

X

For a week, I lived on milk. Each day at noon, I exercised my legs in the woods, going a few steps further at each excursion. The timber was mostly silver birch, but interspersed with young pines and coppiced chastnut trees.

What I thought to be a hunting preserve was, on inspection, a bustling manufactory. At the limit of my strength, I sat down on a tree-stool and smoked a pipe. The cartmen, wood-cutters and foot-passengers at first averted their eyes from the stranger, but one time a lad in green liverie saluted me, and the next day stopped to tell me the weather.

That evening at ten by the clock, I was summoned by Mme de Maurepas. I took care to bring with me my surgical basin, wrapped in a cloth.

She was seated at her escritoire, veil lifted. Her cheeks and neck were horribly marked, but her eyes had lost their glaucous tint. Seated on a tabouret, stitching under the same candle-light, was Mme Nicolette.

"You have done well, madame. And you, also, if I may say so, Mme Nicole."

"So, I shall keep my eye-sight, Colonel Neilson, such as it is?"

"The patches will heal, madame, I promise you."

I put my basin on the table and lifted the cloth.

"What is that, Mr Neilson?"

"It is a culture."

"What are you cultivating?"

Mme de Maurepas recoiled.

"I am cultivating small-pox."

Mme Nicolette screamed.

"By God, you intend to infect my people. Answer me, now, before I call my guard."

"Yes."

"You lost your mind on that disastrous moor."

I waited for science to win out over fear.

"Explain yourself, you villain."

"This disease is an invading host. Here, in this dish, are its scouts, sent forth with half-understood orders and defective arms, easily overpowered and taken into captivity. We read his despatches, break his ciphers, dismantle his weapons to gauge their range and charge. We post pickets at every weak point in the body so that when the enemy's main force arrives, it is ambushed at every defile and river ford, becomes sick and mutinous, and withdraws, burning its supplies, and seeks a weaker adversary."

In the candle-light, the women's faces glistened.

Mme Nicolette peered at the culture. "I do not see your goblin army, Colonel."

"Dearest Marrin," said Mme la marquise. "Colonel Neilson is a soldier and talks as a soldier, his mouth ever full of sieges and battles. It is pleasant to devise a system that appears to reconcile the most jarring and discordant phenomena, but that system arises in our impressions and fancies, and we should never confound it with the real chains that bind Nature's secret operations."

We gauped at Mme la marquise.

"Or so I have read," the lady mumbled.

"Shall you call, madame, your servants and tenants to be inoculated?"

"They will not come and you will destroy my authority."

"You might call on M. le curé."

"Pouf!"

I put down my best card. "Years from now, when this disease is just a memory of old women, they will say: 'It was Mme de Maurepas, a lady of strong parts and unbending will, who introduced inoculation into the Kingdom of France.'"

"What do you require, Colonel Neilson?"

"How many servants has she?"

"Seventeen indoors. Thirty-one out-of-doors."

"And her tenants?"

"Four hundred and twelve."

"All children and invalids comprised?"

"Yes. Yes."

"I ask her to have ordered five hundred needles of Nuremberg steel and two hundred feet of red silk thread.

And silver thimbles, of different sizes so as to suit the fingers of both men and women, five dozen."

"Scissors?"

"One dozen. Also of German steel."

"You shall ruin me." And then: "Granted."

"Now, would you ask Mme Nicole to thread this needle with six inches of thread?" I unwound my tie and lowered my shirt to the elbow.

"Not bad for an old chap, eh, madame?"

"Chush, dear girl."

"Here, exactly here . . ."

"I shall faint."

That seemed improbable.

"Here, I pass the needle under the skin. I pull the thread, leaving one inch showing at each side. Now, I snip the thread and place the needle and the unwanted thread aside to go into the furnace."

I stood up and tied up my shirt. "In the villages of Isfahan, in the kingdom of Persia, which I knew in its ruin, it is the custom for an old woman to pass through the villages, once the summer's heat has abated, crying out for all who wish to be infected. She has with her a dish of—"

"Yes, yes. We know what she has."

"They gather together under a quilt, telling fortunes

and reciting holy stories. They feel unwell, and suffer four or five patches, which leave no trace. We shall see, by experiment, if that is the case in the Christian lands. I ask permission to take my leave. I shall not attend Mme la marquise tomorrow. Or the next day."

"Why red thread, Mr Colonel?"

"So, Mme Nicole, we shall know who has had the treatment. In Persia, where it is the custom of men and women to wear dark and fuscous colours, the thread used is white. Here in France, where the costume is gayer, I thought that red might be more perceivable, so to speak."

XI

I had bolted my door. There was a bustle outside, and Mme la marquise de Maurepas herself appeared, veiled to the nines, in a humour.

"You have four or five patches on your face."

"Also a flux of the bowel, fever, night sweats, aches in the joints and vomiting, both dry and wet. I have noted the symptoms for you, madame."

"You are disgusting."

I said: "I propose a Thursday morning. If Mme la marquise would consent to grant her people rest on Friday and Saturday, the two days' surplus of rest, as well as the Lord's Day, will be sufficient interval for their full recovery."

"Who do you suppose, Colonel Neilson, will on those days milk the cows, make the butter and cream, inspect the fences, collect the eggs, open the sluices, feed the swine and beasts, fold the ewes, answer the correspondence, tend the fires and empty the slop-pails?"

"I shall, my lady."

"If they see me in clogs and carrying hay on my back, they will lose all fear of me."

"They will, my lady."

XII

The day appointed for the inoculation was bright and cold. I had feared none of the people might come, but come they did, the house servants congregating on the terrace between the guard and the kitchens, and the outdoor servants and tenants on the bridge. I had set up my dispensary before the kitchen-steps. Prompt at ten, Mme la marquise came out in a wide hat and veil, attended only by Mme Nicolette. I had placed for her a high-backed chair without arms before the main door. Once she was settled, Mme Nicolette joined me at my station.

Before me, the people were arranged by rank or craft. In front were young men in green, whom I took to be my lady's huntsmen, and beside them, neither quite in front or quite behind, were the coachmen and grooms. Further back, and keeping a good distance from the churls, were the house servants.

"People of La Ferté-Joyeuse!" I shouted and then moderated my tone. "Mme la marquise de Maurepas has called you here for an affair of physick. For some time, Mme la marquise has been afflicted with the small-pox."

There was a gasp, which I thought factitious. I am sure that they very well knew.

"During my campaigns in the King's service in the Indies, I often had the chance to assist at a treatment against the disease, which has been long practised in those parts and is now being introduced into the lands of Christendom." I was on the top of saying that King George of England had had his daughters treated, but thought better of it. Protestant medicine was devilry to these people. "Mme la marquise is now cured of the affliction and wishes that none of you should suffer as she has suffered. The treatment is alike to the engrafting of pear- or plum-trees. A piece of common thread, soaked in alcohol and the medicine, is inserted under the skin of the upper arm. The wound will swell a little, and then itch fit to have you walk upon the ceiling. Some of you may also feel unwell for a day or two days. At that price, you will be safe from the small-pox for as long as you shall live. Just as important, you shall not communicate the distemper to your parents or infants."

Nobody moved or spoke.

From among the horse-men, Pierre Dalouhe sprang to life.

"Friends!" he roared. "Look at this!" He pointed to the twist of red thread on his sleeve. "I am alive and could beat every one of you over fences. The Colonel has seen the world. He has sailed to the Indies, to China and to America. While we know only the church steeple at Bâle and the tap-room at Saint-Véran."

His pleasantry fell flat as a pan-cake. Nobody moved or spoke. Mme la marquise sat.

There was a commotion by the kitchen door, and a squall of slaps and feminine curses. In a body, the hunts-men drove in and pulled out a little windmill. It was my friend the kitchen-maid. She stood trembling half to death before me.

I said: "Please to take charge of the women and girls, Mme Nicolette."

The huntsmen were in a quandary. Their forest honour had obliged them to defend the kitchen-lass, but not to submit to untested surgery. They could not go back, but only forward. A strong young man, who appeared to be their leader, shook down his top-coat. The weather-burned neck and alabaster shoulder brought a gasp from the kitchen-maids and a hiss from the married ladies. His companions formed line behind him.

Then the *hierarchie* or distinction of ranks at La Ferté-Joyeuse, hitherto my enemy, became my friend. If the woods could dare this thing, could the commons drag heels! First came the stables, herded by M. Dalouhe: squire, first equerry, coachman, postilion, harness-maker, saddler, spur-maker; then the mechanics, farrier, carpenters, wheel-wright, brewer, cutler; then stockman, dairymaids, butter-makers and shepherds shaggy and wild as their ewes; behind the herds, at a good distance, head gardener, two under-gardeners and three under-under-gardeners; and now the household: maître d'hôtel, butteler, table officers, four footmen and two pages, sempstress, buttoner, laundress, starcher, house-maids, cooks, kitchen-girls, ice-boy; surgeon and apothecary; old servants in retreat; and finally, by no means to their credit, the men of the guard and their officer.

Still, the tenants did not come forward.

It was now for Mme la marquise to decide. Would she be satisfied with what she had and hope that, at the next visitation, her household might stand safe amid the weeping farms? She sat, immobile, veiled.

There was on the bridge a batch of farmers' wives, in a place that seemed to be theirs by right or immemorial usage. Among them was a lady who must have had a reputation for a wit. She was loud in her sallies but also voluble, for she was at any moment the strongest voice of the majority. At her flanks were two small children, a boy and a girl.

Mme de Maurepas rose and walked towards the bridge. The crowd formed hedges each side of her. She stood before the woman, who dropped a curtesie.

"Mme Porcher, will you permit me?"

She took each child by the hand, and then, with grace, turned about, and offered each the other hand.

"Now which of you good children is to have a sugar-plum?"

Mme Porcher stood, as if frozen, on her spot. Then, taking her skirts in her hands, and looking to heaven, like a queen in England going to the block, she stepped towards her doom. Her sisters and their weans, in some gradation of acreage or length of tenancy too subtle for my understanding, formed line behind her. Their menfolk and lads, with much mobb and banter, pushed the youngest and silliest to the head.

I was weary as I had never been. My ankles were sticks of fire. Looking round, I saw Mme Nicolette asleep on a stool. In her place, the little kitchen-maid was dish-dashing away. I had a mind to lay down and die.

Of the needles, two remained unused. Mme de Maurepas spoke.

"You will oblige me, Col. Neilson, if in your reports on the inoculative treatment to His Majesty and Mr Intendant Debret..."

The people started at those dreadful names.

"... you remark the good conduct of the people of La Ferté-Joyeuse."

There was an attempt at a cheer, but Mme de Maurepas raised her hand. She halted before the kitchen-maid.

"What is your name, servant-girl?"

"Marie-Ange de la Contrition, mum."

"Brave Marie-Ange de la Contrition," Mme la marquise said and walked to the house.

XIII

I was writing by lamp-light the reports Mme de Maurepas had requested, when Mme Nicolette rattled the door to say that Her Ladyship wished me to attend her. It was near midnight. I found Mme la marquise in undress by the fire, unveiled, a shawl on her shoulders, her hair brushed. An embroidered fire-screen shielded her face from the spitting pine.

I knelt before her. "I thank you from my heart, Mme de Maurepas. You have done great service to the King and to those poor people."

"I did not do it for His Majesty or for my people. I did it to save the countenance of the man I have loved for more than half my life."

She was trembling. For the first time in her life, Mme de Maurepas was frightened.

I said: "Come now with me. We have years to make up."

She said: "You will find, sir, that I have not expertise

in such affairs. I was a girl and then a superfluous wife and then a hideous widow. I never learned how to please a man."

"I believe, madame, that between us we shall manage."

In the candle-light, I saw her lovely back. She bent to the floor to retrieve her nightgown.

"You have torn it, you brute."

"It was in my way."

She lay on her side and looked at me. A gash in the lace uncovered her breast. She said: "There are ways, Colonel Neilson, of taking a strong place other than by direct assault. You might have tried stratagem or negociation. You might have said: 'My lady, will you do me the courtesy of taking up your shift?' I suppose that courtship in Scotland is not a prolonged affair?"

"Cannot Mme Nicolette repair it?"

"How can I chide my maid for biding out late with the second groom if she sees her mistress taking her pleasure with the first Scottish soldier to call at her house? No, you have made of me a sempstress, as was always your intention, and then, you blackguard, you bought up and destroyed every sewing-needle in the Generality."

"Madame de Maurepas, you have within your breast a

conscience who is my sworn enemy. She says to you: 'If you let this man please you even for an instant, you shall never hear the end of it.' I cannot negociate with her. I can only overpower her.

"Tomorrow, she will come to you in her hat and travelling clothes and say: 'Since you are a-gandygoing with this gentleman in your chamber, I shall consider myself dismissed. I shall expect my arrerages of salary and the punctual payment of the 3 per cent life annuity you were kind enough to constitute at the Paris Town House. If you do not wish me to walk to my sister at Blois, you may order Dalouhe to harness the cart.'

Mme de Maurepas sat up. She said: "Madame de la Pudeur, you are the oldest of my servants and the most faithful. Many times, you have saved me from error. Yet you presume too much. I remind you that, during my illness, which you counselled me to bear in silence, Colonel Neilson took steps to save my eye-sight, my life and my estate. You must permit me to join the main stream of our sex and enjoy those sensations of happiness that alone make the feminine existence supportable. I would have you remember that love is the consolation not just of light, but of honest women also. Am I, by reason of my rank, to be denied the joy of a miller's wife? On the sparse occasions when I have a mind to *engandigouiller* with Mr Neilson, I would have you retire to your chamber to rest."

Mme de Maurepas seemed delighted with her firm, but kindly, tone. She said: "Why do you look at my breast, Mr Neilson?"

"Because he has an interesting shape."

"You may touch him, if you wish, and his companion."

"I shall try this time to be less rough."

"Heavens! One may do it again?"

"Let us make the attempt."

"If you wish. But . . ."

"But what?"

". . . but this. The place is more sparsely defended than your scouts led you to believe. In such circumstances, Colonel Neilson, a prudent officer will leave a portion of his force in reserve."

Mme de Maurepas had abandoned the shreds of her gown. We lay together, as naked as new-borns, touching from forehead to toe. We were as different one from the other as it was possible to be. It occurred to me that such a want of symmetry might be the force or principle that runs through nature and permits her to persist and adjust to the revolutions of time.

She said: "A woman might never tire of such happiness."

I said: "Jeanne-Alexandrine-Clothilde de La Vrillière Joyeuse de Joyeuse, marquise de Maurepas, Charlevoix and Bercy, and comtesse and baronne of many other fine places, will you have the good nature to marry me?"

Mme de Maurepas yawned. "So! Not content with enjoying her person, he now wishes to possess her lands."

"On the contrary, should he have the good fortune to be so honoured, he renounces for all time his husband's right or *jus mariti* over her manors, lordships, dwelling-houses, fortalices, farms, granges, woods, ponds, weirs, sluices, policies, shops, goods, securities, capitals, cargoes, rents, moveables, cash, chattels, gold, silver, gems, loans, annuities (both for life and perpetual), shares, actions, effects, assurances and everything else without exception, all and severally, whether in the Kingdom of France or oversea. His colonel's half-pay, should it ever please His Very Christian Majesty to pay it, shall more than suffice his elementary needs."

Lulled by her property, Mme de Maurepas was falling into sleep. Her eyes opened and then closed. From the frontier of sleep, she said: "Refused."

A FOUNDLING

XIV

At the milking next morn, a public had gathered to watch Her Ladyship attend her friend Mouron. The beast's milking-maid, aghast at losing her charge, quivered in a hot red ball of fever and misery. Mme la marquise de Maurepas stood up, turned over the girl's hands, inspected them for cleanliness, and relinquished cow and stool.

The worst labour was the sluice-gates on the river. Mme de Maurepas was experimenting a new rural system, in which she would flood for an hour an expanse of haughs or water-meadows so as to give her beasts a precocious bite of grass and have them early to market. By good fortune M. Dalouhe, who had two days' advance in the small-pox treatment, saw me at work and added his shoulder to the wheel.

A scrap of Virgil flittered through my head: *Claudite iam rivos, pueri; sat prata biberunt.*" I said: "Close up the dykes, lads! The fields have drunk their fill."

At noon, I joined my lady in the cart which she had filled from the stooks in the hay-house. In the wagon's lee, Mme Nicolette was asleep.

"I am lying down in this vehicle, Mr Neilson, not out of wantonness but from inanition. Be your age."

"We have lost nineteen years of happiness. We must try and live those years, if only in a sort of echo or mimic."

Mme la marquise's face and neck were burned from the wind. She said: "On the île de France, I dreamed that you and I would slip away and live among the blacks on their rock. You would teach them how to cast cannon and fight in formation. I would learn their languages and write down their songs. I wanted to be a good wife. I felt so deep in sin . . ."

"Yes, so much better to send me in irons to Pondicherry."

"I wished to save your life. I had despaired of my own. I could see that you would fight the Chevalier Durfort. I said to Mr Maurepas that if you fell in single combat, the blacks would rise and, to avenge you, kill every French man, woman and child in the île de France. He was afeared of the blacks."

"But that day of the fête, you took my pistols, so I could not defend myself!"

"I am sorry, Mr Neilson, but I needed them. Mr Chevalier Durfort was in love with one of the ladies of the island, but it never hurts to be prudent."

I was struck dumb. Then I remembered how the

Chevalier and Mme Patelin had danced the strathspey, after many hours of rehearsal.

"Captain Béranger was kind enough to write me of your fair conduct on the campaign of *L'Atalante*. He was again at Pondicherry, in 'Thirty-three or 'Thirty-four, and gave me an account of the fight at Gingie Fort. Then my lord died and I was much in business, and had no news of you till the gazettes arrived with the letters from Scotland that said you had fallen in glory with your Irish men. I became ill and then very ill."

My world was transfigured. All those weary years in India and Persia, when to myself I was alone, Jeanne de Joyeuse stood at my shoulder, like the goddess that protects and guides the warrior on the plain of Troy.

"I had given Mr Durfort the wherewithal to buy a regiment. He did not do so but spent the money, as was his right, on dowries for his two sisters. He had learned English, I think for love of you, and for that reason was sent into Scotland with Prince Charles Edward."

"I cannot describe to you the grace and courage of the Chevalier's last moments in the battle on the moor. He saved the life of the Prince of Wales."

"Many good men fell that day. Thank God that the best man was preserved."

"My lady, I do not share your esteem for the Prince of Wales."

"I did not mean the Prince of Wales."

From the parish church tower, the Angélus inundated the cold sky.

I said: "When he has fed the beasts, does she wish him to examine her people?"

"No. She shall do so."

"They will not be in the most agreable of humours."

"Her maidservant will attend her."

XV

The inoculation against the small pox caused a vibration in the balance of force at La Ferté-Joyeuse.

Mme Nicolette ruled the bedchamber and her lover the commons and outer courtyard. Marie-Ange de la Contrition, the foundling from the Hôtel-Dieu of Orléans, was the heiress of below-stairs. (For, surely Madame la marquise's favour, conferred in so very public a fashion, must one day be matched by a dowry!) Rising two hours before dawn, she found the kitchen stoves lit and the chamber-pots emptied. The poor girl could not reach for a pail or brush but it was taken from her. Not a day passed without that a coney, or a brace of partridges, or a string of larks, was laid at the scullery door for her particular table while a youth in new forest green simpered at the pump. As for Manon Porcher, wife of the tenant-farmer at La Borie, she let fall by leaden hints that the marquise had concerted strategies with her afore-hand. When Mme Nicolette conveyed that, Mme la marquise burst into laughter, which I had not heard from her since the île de France.

The proprietrix's labour in field and bower and grange, far from diminishing her in the eyes of her people, made her the more dreadful. Her servants thought she employed them because she was lazy, for that it is what they wanted to be. Madame la marquise's scientific inquiries and her far-flung correspondence were mere aspects of her idleness. When they saw she could do all that they did, not well, but not badly, while the wounded soldier did the man's work, like-wise, they felt unsafe in their places.

Two servants had missed the inoculation. M. Ballin, my lady's factor or intendant, had been that day on her business in Orléans. Mme de Maurepas became pensive.

After a period, she said: "That is his choice, and I shall not press him. The variable we are here testing is not M. Ballin's affection, but the efficiency of the inoculative treatment." Then she added, as to herself: "The other variable shall be put to separate experiment."

The second absent was Mme Plaie. That lady had been the nurris or wet-nurse of the late Duke in his infancy and lived alone in a bothy in the woods. Neither the caresses of Mme de Maurepas, nor the magnificent apartment prepared for the dame in the castle, could unstick her from her tumblewrack nest. The daily tramp with her dinner, half a league there and a half-league back, with a ragging in the middle, fell by its own gravity on the foundling, who also aired and swept the den. Since Mme Plaie would admit none but her little favourite, and the child was inoculated, Mme de Maurepas was content to leave matters as they were.

For the district, it was most vexing. God would punish Mme de Maurepas for her pride and her Devil's sciences, that was sure, but why was He taking his time? He had started well enough, in visiting on her a terrible scourge, but now it seems she has scarcely a patch. She has taken up with her physician, a Scottish man of unbridled ferocity who (it was said) had killed in single combat thirty-seven men (and two women), which tally caused the ladies' husbands to ponder and be backward in conversation.

XVI

I had about my neck a stone that wearied me but, like Sisyphus, I could not put it down. It was an unblemished diamond of 490 carats' weight. I had received it, in its rough state, from my beloved friend and spiritual guide, Father Patrick O'Crean, at the moment that our vessel, the *Prince-de-Conty*, wrecked off the île de France (which the Dutchmen call Mauritius) in the year 1727. His last injunction to me was that I should polish it and give it to the King, his master. The King was James Stuart, who had been taken as a babe when his father escaped from London in the Revolution of 1688, and was living in exile in Rome.

By birth and temperament, I was no Jacobite and I confess that I dawdled at my solemn task. In India, the stone was notorious and there were men a-plenty who, had they known it was about my throat, would have cut that useful artery. I dared not have it polished in any of the jewel-places of the half-continent. By the greatest good fortune, while on embassy for our East India Company in Persia in 1740, I found, in the famous city of Isfahan, an old man who with the worst grace imaginable shaped it into the most perfect jewel that exists on the surface of the earth. Believing that King James had joined the expedition to Scotland in 'Forty-five, I had taken ship for Inverness and there, in the battle on Culloden Moor, destroyed my command and my memory.

In this amnesian state, I had come into the Sologne, found my mistress dying of the small-pox and her house in insurrection. I could not, in justice, abandon my lady in that crisis for the sake of a cause that I detested and believed long lost. Only once Mme de Maurepas were restored in health and authority could I think of setting out for the Stuart Court at Rome.

"Mr Neilson! Where are you?"

"Forgive me, madame. I was dreaming."

"I fear I am no sort of company for you, Mr Neilson. I must call on re-inforcement."

Mme de Maurepas looked into the distance at her troops passing in review. "The committee for the restoration of the convent at Les Thelles will meet here tomorrow. Will you not help me entertain those pious matrons?"

"It will be an honour for me, my lady, and an edification."

"Or it may be that your taste turns to literature. M. l'abbé Longue at Romorantin has composed a Latin epic on the defence of Louisbourg in ten thousand hexameters."

"I shall listen with attention to some or even all of that mighty work."

"Or what about some of our sportsmen? Once, in the Low Navarre, M. le baron Jaseur killed a timber wolf with but his teeth. He has many such stories."

"I will value each hour in the company of so famous a Nimrod."

"Mr Neilson, you do not seem to be very sociable."

XVII

"You are out of sorts, my lady."

"I am not out of sorts, whatever that means. I am never out or in of sorts."

I wondered what had occurred. Mme la marquise's skin had a clearer aspect. Her eyes were bright. It was not a post day. Nothing had happened that morning but the visit of the devout ladies.

Mme de Maurepas said: "Mme de Rabutin does not permit herself even innocent pleasures."

They want me out of here. Now, why should those feminine saints wish to see the back of me? I said:

"I believe, madame, that my presence here is an inconvenience to you. Until I have recovered my mobility, and can continue into Italy, will you not let me occupy some cottage or workman's shade in your woods?"

"You have no servant, Mr Neilson."

"I am accustomed to living alone so that, when you visit, as I would have you do as often as you find convenient, you shall not craunch on rabbit-bones or catch your skirts on a floor-nail. Like all soldiers, I am a capable cook, baker, sewer and cobbler. The open air will aid your recovery."

"But who shall dress me?"

"I imagine we shall live in our linen."

"Who shall darn my stockings and seam my chemise?"

"I shall."

"Truly, Colonel, your courage has not been exaggerated. I would have you promise not to call me Cynisca or Amaryllis. For a fighting soldier, you have a sore weakness for the idyllic."

"I promise."

Mme de Maurepas thought for a while. She said: "Prudence de Joyeuse hid her lover in the woods."

"There, then. You have your authority."

"The count her husband fed them both to his boar-hounds."

"I am sorry, madame."

"Thank you. The incident occurred in the reign of Philip the Fair, and the elapse of four hundred and fifty years has not abated its evil. May I consider your woodland project, which sounds delicious, and return you answer this evening?"

Which was a refusal.

Mme de Maurepas said: "There is disaffection in the house and in the fields in which, I am sorry to say, my neighbours are intermeddling. I would wish to have so famous a warrior at my side. My own retired habit of life has made me careless of your entertainment. The late duke my father bought several thousand of fine Burgundy wine and forgot to drink them. They are for you. As for his library, where you may champ and browse to your heart's content, my father did not care to read but liked, as it were, to have good authors look at him. If you care to hunt or fish, my woods, river and ponds and my hounds and hunt-servants are at your disposal. I ask only that each night at ten you come to my bedchamber to receive my blessing for the night. Should you wish to stay with me, I am at your service. Do you like tea?"

"No."

"Nor do I. What do you like?"

"I like you, Mme de Maurepas."

"And I like you, Mr Neilson. You shall have Champagne. Champagne never hurt anybody."

"Do you have family, Mr Neilson?"

"The Neilsons have been in Scotland some time. A Neilson commanded the Pictish centre at the battle of Mons Graupius in, I think, Anno Domini Eighty-three. I recollect reading that in Tacitus' life of his father-in-law Julius Agricola."

Mme de Maurepas looked evil.

That after-dinner, as I was wrestling in the library with an Arabic manual of physick, Mme de Maurepas tip-taed in.

"Oh! You are at your Arabs. I shall come back at another time."

"May I not take down what you require?"

"It is not important. I was looking for a book in English." And then, at the door, turning: "On trade."

When I called on Mme de Maurepas after supper, she was smiling. She said: "I happened to be in my library, Colonel Neilson, and coming by chance on a Tacitus, I found to my surprise that there is no mention of a Neilson at the battle of Mons Graupius, a.d. 83."

"Forgive me, madame. I suppose it is one of those legends that persist in ancient families though they have no written authority."

Mme la marquise de Maurepas seemed unprepared for capitulation in so pressing an affair. "No doubt," she said. "I never accepted that a Joyeuse was present at the Incarnation. What we may agree is that the house of Neilson, though evidently of some little age, emerges from the mist of Scotland only after the county of Joyeuse had already passed its brilliant meridian."

"I am sure that is the case."

I thought: This lady is wondering if she should marry. She is, as it were, clearing some of the rubble strewn across the way to the altar.

"Let us speak of something else, dear Colonel. I detest pride of family."

"I could not agree more, my lady."

While I liked Mme de Maurepas as she was, with nothing to be added and, God knows, nothing to be taken away, she wished with me to straighten an edge here, there square off a corner, throw out a window above, brick up a door below. For Mme la marquise de Maurepas, a Scotsman was just a Frenchman at a more primitive stage of formation.

XVIII

The inoculation had been but a first skirmish. My strength, consisting of Mme Nicolette and M. Dalouhe, and the orphan Marie-Ange de la Contrition, comprised the pick or flower of the field, but could bear no casualty. Against me were the upper servants and farm-tenants and, at their head, M. Ballin, who feared for his place and, no doubt, hoped to profit from the dispersion of the lands at the death of his childless mistress and make his own estate in a corner of it.

That gentleman called on me. As he was too fine to enter my chamber, I came out onto the stair-landing. He had, it seems, orders to improve my accommodations. He was a man of the middle age, a town-body rather than a country-man, well-dressed but not too well-dressed, and well-spoken likewise. I could see that he wished to have my measure, as we say, but was too cautious to pass beyond generalities. To reassure him, I said that as a soldier I was long accustomed to live without a man-servant; and especially, I said only to myself, one detached by M. Ballin to spy on me. As I did not expect to weary Mme la marquise for much longer, but go into Italy whither I was commanded, I saw no purpose in the trouble and expense of renewing the late duke's apartments.

As I penetrated the economy of La Ferté-Joyeuse, I found much to surprise me. Mme la marquise had fewer allies than appeared. At moments of temporarie difficulty, her father had been wont to sell offices in his household for ringing cash. The consequence was that some of the lady's higher servants were not servants at all, but cits from Orléans or further distant. For an annuity of immaculate credit, the privilege of calling on Mme la marquise on New Year's Day, and the right to parade about the place and give orders when she were absent, a master of appeals was her Grand Steward, an agent of change her Chief of Venerie, and a tanner in retreat her Master of Horse. The boobies could not be dismissed but only bought out, which Mme la marquise did not seem especially eager to enterprise.

Mme Nicolette, as Mme la marquise's confidante-in-love, was now out of my reach and I no more spoke to her than to the Queen of France. That was a pity for I rather wished to know what prices were now on offer against Mme de Maurepas taking husband. M. Dalouhe was under her orders. That left only Miss Marie-Ange, but the lass was more than enough. No officer ever had a better intelligencer.

Mme la marquise's favour, and her shy sylvan lovers, had not so much turned the foundling's head as planted in it a sense of worth. With the elevation of Mme Nicolette, the orphan alone now waited on me in my chamber. To recover my High-School Greek, and to deflect somewhat the child's interrogatory, I was reading Lucian's *Dialogues of the Sea-Gods* (in-folio, Florence, 1496) which was already well-stained with blancmange.

"May I speak, sir?"

"Of course, mademoiselle."

"Do you love Her Ladyship, sir?"

"I do, Mlle Marie-Ange. I have loved her since I was just sixteen years old."

"But that is ages!"

"Indeed, mademoiselle."

"Oh, sir, I should so very much like to be loved when I am all-grown."

Struck dumb, I reached for the bottle. It was torn from my hand. The red wine splashed the in-folio.

"Only I am to pour your wine! Her Ladyship says!"

"I am sorry, mademoiselle, for my presumption."

"I am to take the bottle from the cellar myself, and pour only from a bottle I have opened by my hand. The same with your cider and eau-de-vie."

"Of course," I said. "And it is you I must thank for this excellent Solognote pie?"

"Yes. I am not to leave the fire even for an instant while it is cooking. I am to bake your bread and taste your milk and draw your beer and myself select the eggs for your brioche. The eggs must be complete and have no blemish."

"Her Ladyship has great faith in you, mademoiselle."

"And if I do for Her Ladyship this one small thing, I am excused all other duties apart from Mme Plaie and am to have wages of twenty sols a day, including Sunday, and cloth for a new dress and cap at Whitsun and Michaelmas, and Her Ladyship will teach me to read and write and, if at night I am frightened, I may . . ."

The lass stopped. That was a secret too great even for her friend the Colonel.

"Mlle Marie-Ange, you may say to me whatever you

wish, but I would prefer that you did not talk of your appointments to the other servants."

"I don't care. When Her Ladyship had no friends, it was I, not they, who stood up for her, though I was frightened to death. And that is why I am to have twenty sols a day, including Sunday, and cloth for a new dress and cap at Whitsun and Michaelmas and . . . I don't care for them a straw. I don't care that you have bewitched Her Ladyship and will turn us all out and give our places to Protesters."

Mlle Marie-Ange paused. "Sir, what are Protesters?"

"I am the worst person to inform you, mademoiselle. Have you asked Her Ladyship?"

"Her Ladyship says I may ask her but one question each week and that only on Sunday. I have my question for this Sunday."

Mlle Marie-Ange blushed down to her bare feet.

"It's not my business, young miss, and do not take this as an impudence, but I believe Her Ladyship wishes you to wear shoes all the time, and not solely in her presence."

"But they will become worn and stained!"

"Ah, I had not thought of that."

XIX

The next morning, Mlle Marie-Ange came in, dropped the trey she had in her hands, and burst into tears. She made to run away, but I caught her, set her in my chair, and untangled a story from her.

I dragged her in a greet to Mme la marquise's bedroom. That lady looked up from her writing.

"Is it not my brave friend, Marie-Ange de la Contrition? But you are sad. Come to me, dear. Mr Neilson, will you not bring for the child a tabouret?"

Marie-Ange sat down, stood up, sat down again. She looked at Mme de Maurepas and looked away. She opened her mouth but no sound emerged.

"Would you like to hold my hand, child?"

The lass took out her hand, as if from a wrapping-cloth, then put it back again. She lowered her head.

"Perhaps, dear child, Mr Neilson may tell your story."

The kitchen maid nodded in a rain of tears.

I made a precise or summary of what the child had told me.

"What are your duties now, my puppet?"

"The Colonel's dinner..."

"You are excused. Mr Neilson shall dine with me."

". . . and Mme Plaie."

Mme de Maurepas hissed. It seemed Mme Plaie's brief seventeenth-century labour had been more than rewarded in sixty years of tyranny.

"I shall myself take Mme Plaie her milk-soupe."

"My lady, I believe there should be no alteration in the child's ordinair course of life or routine."

Mme de Maurepas looked at me as if I had spoken in Turkish.

I said: "The child shall be overlooked every step of the way to the bothy and back. With your permission, I shall not dine with you; but, again with your consent, shall call on your hunt servants." I had no faith in my lady's guard. While entirely useless, they would also make a bustle.

"I shall accompany you. Marrin, have them make up a bed for the child in my cabinet. And they are to furnish her with a new dress and cap and slippers for her feet. Also a night-gown."

"Yes, my lady. Come with me, marmote."

At the door, Miss Marie-Ange turned and spoke. "When Mr Colonel has killed that man, I shall go back to the Hospital."

"You shall not, child, so long as I am living, or Mr Neilson."

Mme de Maurepas was looking at me.

"Please speak, Mr Neilson. Say anything."

"Might the man not be her father?"

"Oh, Mr Neilson, can you not bring me her dossier from my cabinet? It shall be under H for Hospital."

Mme de Maurepas's records were, as I expected, in good order. The bundle had but a few items.

"Will you not read them to me, Mr Neilson? My eyesight was never of the best and has not been improved by the small-pox."

"The first item is a report from Sr Marguerite Ganeau of the Carmélite sisters at Orléans and concerns a child found on the step of the cathedral of La-Sainte-Croix on December 25, 1736. With it is a copy of the child's certificate of baptism, of that same holy date."

"The sisters baptise the foundlings at once for fear they should die."

"The second is a letter to Mlle Glason, superior of the Hôtel-Dieu of Orléans from Mme Modelle, abbess of the convent at Thelles, dated January 1, 1744."

I read: "Her demeanour is always unrecollected. She laughs when she should be sad and weeps when she should feel blessed. She has not the smallest idea of discipline. She is, I believe, unsuited as much to the contemplative life as to the regularity of a closed house."

"Please stop. Of all my relations, Mme de Thelles is, against vigorous competition, the stupidest."

"The next item, which carries no date, is a memorial for His Majesty on the project of sending disorderly women from the metropolis to Guyane …

"Now where are we? Marie-Anne Furet, assassination. Anne Berthaut, infanticide. Louyse Scarron, disorderly conduct. Anne Monart, counterfeiting. Berthe Lagarde, harlotry."

"Stop!"

"Here. The named Marie-Ange de la Contrition. Aged about nine years. Rebellion."

Mme de Maurepas seemed crushed.

"The last is a state of the property of the named Marie-Ange de la Contrition on leaving the Hospital into the service of Mme de Maurepas on November 11, 1746. One dress, one cap. Value: four and one half sols."

"Save her, Mr Neilson."

XX

I thought of asking Mme de Maurepas not to accompany me, for I feared she would attract the attention of her servants to what I wished should not be observed. But she was so wild and agitated, I thought better to have her in my view.

The huntsmen's earth or sett was at the head of the eastern commons. The room was as busy as a fabrick. In one corner, where the hind-quarters of an old horse hung from a hook, one young man was cutting collops for the hounds. Another was hurch'd over a brasier, casting bullets. A third was greasing gun-stocks. All were standing. At a desk was the sunburnt young man from the inoculation, who was writing with ease and appeared to be the leader of the company. Mme de Maurepas looked round.

"Now, where is M. Duclos?"

"I am here, my lady."

"Your father taught me to shoot the cross-bow. From you, I need a service of incomparably greater importance. Colonel Neilson, would you kindly explain?"

I said: "Mme la marquise de Maurepas has reason to believe that there is a design of violence against one of her kitchen servants, the foundling Marie-Ange de la Contrition. To-day at noon, as the lass was carrying Mme Plaie's dinner to the cottage, at a point beside the fallen ash-tree, she was approached by a richly dressed young gentleman mounted on a bay horse."

The young man's eyes flickered. Four of the lads vanished into air.

"The gentleman reached down and handed her a bunch of yellow flowers. The lass let them fall. The man laughed and cantered away."

"In which direction, sir?"

"To the south. Towards the house."

I glanc'd round. The room had emptied. There was just the three of us.

"My lady, I would counsel you to appoint M. Duclos to command this campaign. I am an elephant in woods."

"But what shall you do, M. Duclos?"

I intervened: "Madame, generals do not speak of their movements until they are completed."

Mme de Maurepas flushed and then brought herself under control. "Good," she said. "I am glad that Mr Neilson is here to remind me of the military etiquette. At least, I have shown with my feminine outburst how very important this matter is to me."

She turned and walked out. I caught her at the bridge. She had an evil look. I forestalled her.

"There will be a time, my lady, for you to scold me, but it is not now. You must set up your general quarter. Unless, you wish to receive those boys in your bedroom..."

Mme de Maurepas looked bewildered.

I plunged on. "May I suggest your laboratory?"

"Yes."

XXI

I was in my room when, as from the panling, M. Duclos stood before me. He made to speak but I raised my hand.

"Her Ladyship will receive you in her work-room."

"I am not dressed!"

"Nothing like that matters, M. Duclos. What matters is to save the child's life."

In my lady's laboratory, a bench had been cleared. The young men laid out their spoils in a sequence while M. Duclos, by casting glances into retorts and other extempore looking-glasses, sought to make himself presentable. Mme de Maurepas, when she entered, had regained her self-command. M. Duclos began his speech.

"There are hoof-marks, which are unfamiliar to us, and may very well belong to the gentleman's horse."

"May I interject here, my lady?"

M. Duclos turned to me.

"Can you, M. Duclos, make a cast of the shoe-prints?"

"The sand is too loose to take wax."

Mme de Maurepas said: "I shall order the place to be guarded so that they not be obliterated."

"Again, my lady, may I suggest that nothing be done to draw attention to the occurrence?" I turned to M. Duclos. "Shall you take M. Fougue to the place so he make an iron of that type? Or, better, several?"

"If Her Ladyship commands."

I said: "Is it the practice for tenant farmers in this country to shoe their horses?"

M. Duclos said nothing.

After an age, Mme de Maurepas said: "No."

She turned back to M. Duclos. I resolved to hold my tongue.

"Here are the flowers. They have been stepped on by the gentleman's horse."

Mme de Maurepas put on her eye-glasses. "It is late in the year for primroses. Now what is it about primroses?"

M. Duclos blirted: "The girl was frightened to death."

"How do you know, M. Duclos?"

The huntsman stared at his feet.

"Oh, poor child. Poor child."

M. Duclos looked at me in despair. I thought: So I am of some service, after all!

I said: "Mme la marquise de Maurepas wishes to hear everything."

"There were two men concealed in ambush on the east side of the ride."

Mme de Maurepas began to totter. I took a step to catch her, but she recovered herself.

M. Duclos lost his thread. "Fern-stems. Bread-crumbs. Sausage-case."

"Thank you, M. Duclos. This room is now under your direction. You and your men may come here at any time of day or night. You may command from my people anything you need."

"Thank you, my lady."

When we were alone, Mme de Maurepas was sombre.

She said: "This affair is all my occupation." She smiled. "I believe that His Holiness and the King of Prussia will be happy to be spared my Thursday letter, but you, my dearest friend..."

Bloody hell!

"I am sure, my lady, that you must attend to Mlle Marie-Ange."

"Do not think, for a moment, Mr Neilson, that, in this emergency, there is any abatement in my esteem for you or my pleasure in your notice. It was you who taught me to love. Now, I cannot stop."

Mme de Maurepas turned to me with swimming eyes.

"I never truly loved her, Colonel, until I saw the extent of her property." Mme de Maurepas smiled. "In that, Mr Neilson, I am a true daughter of France."

I woke before dawn to sounds beneath my window. In the glimmer, I saw below me Mme de Maurepas, in boots and galbardine, and M. Dalouhe leading a horse packed on both flanks. There was a ringing and tinkling as from glass. M. Duclos was in front, with two leished scent-hounds somewhat resembling our Scotch blood-hounds: always of service in botanical jaunts.

XXII

For Mme de Maurepas, it was a new style of working. She had been used all her life to giving orders and having them executed. She had now a sort of state-major, each man and Mme Nicole intent on a single task in a room flittering with maps and drawings. Each morning and evening, M. Duclos gave a summary or recension of what (if anything) had been achieved. He gave no orders. Tasks found their way to the person most able to fulfil them.

My lady seemed bewildered. She said to me: "I wished to be Rotrude de Joyeuse, in breast-plate and greaves, leading her men to death in the ravines of Rencesvals. Instead, I write circular letters to His Majesty's Intendants."

Primroses they had found, though I had to extract that from M. Dalouhe. From her botanising as a young girl, Mme de Maurepas remembered a damp bank at the northern edge of her woods where a few flowers might still hold up their heads in late March. On the road about one hundred yards distant, there were signs of the passage of a horse and rider. I suggested, aside, to M. Duclos that he prepare for Her Ladyship a chart of the larger proprieties in the northern quarters of La Ferté-Joyeuse.

"Why should Her Ladyship require that, M. Neilson?"

"As a favour to me."

M. Duclos did not trust me. That did not matter. What mattered was that he did not trust Mme la marquise. Mme la marquise trusted nobody, not even Mme Nicolette. Beset on every side by secrets, the inquiry could not advance but stamped up and down like a sick animal. It was only with the utmost blandishment that I extracted from M. Duclos his plan of the district, and the names of the principal proprietors.

In the garden, where we took a turn together, Mme de Maurepas said:

"Why should that horse-man, who he may be so ever, wish to frighten me?"

It was not you he wished to frighten, madame.

"Oh, I am so self-conceited. It was not me that man wished to bully, but you. The whole house saw you and the foundling were friends. How he thought he could affright a man who charged the English guns on Culloden Moor alone—"

"I did not charge. I walked."

"... as I say, alone, is beyond my understanding." Mme de Maurepas smiled at me. "Mr Neilson, historic truth is shallow and misleading. Only legend can truly measure your exploits."

"That day on the Moor, I had nobody I cared about, not even myself. Since then, I have discovered fear. Fear for you and fear for the foundling. I wonder, my lady, if fear and happiness may not be aspects of an identity that cannot be described in the language of appearances."

"Fie, Mr Neilson, I did not know you were a metaphysician. I believe you should have said so before you debauched me from my duty. Can you not be a rough and unlettered soldier?"

"Of course. It is my natural or primeval state."

XXIII

For myself, I observed Mme Nicolette. A soldier is ever alert to disaffection. Her place as Mme la marquise's favourite was not so much threatened as overrun. Yet, as far as I could judge, there was no alteration in her conduct before Mme la marquise, the foundling or me. I cursed that I knew so little of women. I did know that Mme Nicolette very much liked M. Dalouhe and surely wished to have him for husband. The favourising of Miss Marie-Ange might kill two birds with a single stone, for now Mme Nicolette might marry her jo but not leave Mme la marquise destitute of a feminine companion. That conclusion was so favourable to the happiness of the house that I thoroughly distrusted it, and remained as alert as I might be.

Our inquiries were not advancing. It was necessary that I take a more active part.

I have spoken already of the île de France, where, on my voyage to Bengale in the year 1727, I was ship-wrecked. A runaway slave named François Delacour plucked me from the waves, and gave up his life to carry me to Port-Louis, which passed for a settlement in that place.

I had seen my lady once before, as a young girl, in the shareholders' gallery of the Royal Bank at Paris on December 10, 1720, the night the bank stopped. I now found her married, and most displeased to see me. Her husband, M. le marquis de Maurepas, had been appointed governor of that forlorn island and its sister, île Bourbon. He had hoped to make a fortune there, but found that there was no fortune to be made in the waste of water and lianes and scarce bread to be eaten. As far as I could judge before Mme de Maurepas sent me away, their marital relation was not of the easiest. At the death of M. le marquis in 'Thirty-two, and no sign or symptom of a successor, Mme la marquise had herself taken over the administration of the islands, which she managed with a much greater economy than had her lord.

Once I had, against the prevailing winds, doubled the Cape and conveyed Mme la marquise to Port-Louis, I animadverted to my friendship with Mme de Bussy, a near relation of hers whom she had brought from the metropolis to serve as *dame d'atour,* or lady-in-waiting. I believed that Mme de Maurepas, on their return to the old France, would have set the good woman at ease and nearby, but not too much nearby.

"Why on earth do you want to call on Mme de Bussy? Really, William, in the midst of our misfortune!"

"She was kind to me on the island. What little I have by way of address, I owe entirely to the tutelage of Mme la comtesse de Bussy. She will surely have heard that I am in the district."

Mme de Maurepas looked at me as if I were from the Indian Ocean, or further distant, and then slid back into her melancholy. "I forgot to say that I brought your hardes back with me from the island. There was a book, if I remember."

"My journal of the navigation of the *Prince-de-Conty* and an account of the ship-wreck. I cannot thank you enough."

Mme de Maurepas was not listening. She said: "There shall be some early fruits in the glass-house. Will you be so kind as to take Mme de Bussy a basket from me?"

XXIV

La Sologne extends to some two hundred and fifty square leagues, from Orléans in the north to Vierzon in the south, and from Gien in the east to Blois in the west. It is shaped somewhat like a turned-up bowl, the loop of the Loire making the round top and the Cher the flat bottom. The district is poor, or, as the French say, sad. Only the highway from Paris to Toulouse, which runs straight as a Roman soldiers' road from Orléans to Vierzon, is paved but not maintained in good repair.

Outside my lady's Paradise, and away from the valley of the Sauldre, was a waste of scrog birches, whins and heather. The ruts in the road were deep in water. The few houses were of wood, the posts exposed (as in England)

and the interstices plastered with mud. The rooves were thatched with reed and the barns boarded. I saw no window-glass. The pastures were over-run with whins and rushes or, in the dry places, heath as high as a man's waist where burry sheep bumped and burrowed for a blade of grass. Yellow broom and white thorn bushes relieved the eye. The poor Scotsman in me felt quite at home.

A little beyond the hamlet of La Levaille, behind a fence of white pales, was a slate cottage with a thatched roof and a smoking chimney. As I opened the wicket-gate and crossed the close, a squadron of geese ran at me, commanding with hisses and snaps my passeport. At the door, where a honeysuckle was putting out her flowers, there stood a pretty girl in sabots and behind her was my friend, a little gone in age.

"Mme la marquise de Maurepas has commissioned me to bring you the first apricots from La Ferté."

Mme de Bussy smiled. "The ship-wrecked boy has become a great man."

"Nonsense, madame. But he is quite as devoted to you as Mme la gouvernante."

Indoors, as my eyes adjusted to the light of a single window, I saw that all the chairs and horizontale surfaces were occupied by animals, while serins and doves flittered about the upper storey. Mme de Bussy dislodged a fox-cub from an elbow chair. I chose to remain standing and, after a struggle of reciprocal courtesies, the canine returned to his place.

"Ombéline, kindly draw for the Colonel a jug of cider."

"And the new cheese, mum?"

"If it is set."

Mme de Bussy sat down and took up her work. She said:

"I am sure you did not come only to bring me fruits, Mr Neilson."

"Not only. As you may know, Mme de Bussy, I am staying at La Ferté-Joyeuse as Mme la marquise's guest."

"So that is what it is called."

I saw that age, or solitude, or some old resentment of Mme de Maurepas, had curdled Mme de Bussy's famous kindness. I pressed ahead.

"As you will also know, Mme la marquise has for some time been unwell though she is now, thank God, fully recovered."

Mme de Bussy looked down at her work. She might have said: I am waiting, Colonel.

"During her illness, some person or persons sowed dissension in the household which I do not wish to go any further. I asked myself if you, as Mme la marquise's confidante and friend, had heard anything of that character."

"Not at all. I have not seen Mme la marquise since last midsummer."

"Who, madame, is M. le comte de Luynes?"

"I did not know you cared for property, Colonel Neilson."

"I do not, Mme de Bussy. I have none and wish for none."

"M. Luynes is a young man who owns the small estate of Vaultrien, some ten or twelve miles in a northward direction from La Ferté, but passes his time at Paris. He is, like you, in the King's service. He is on half-pay, not because of his youth but because he is a quite exceptionally bad subject. He is Mme la marquise's second cousin. Why do you ask, Mr Neilson?"

At that moment, the girl called Ombéline backed into the room, burdened with provisions. We paused, so that I might take refreshment. As I tasted the ambrosial fare at a side-table, four cats sat poised on their haunches to supply my smallest need. A calling dove took station on Mlle Ombéline's cap.

It seemed I had to give more to receive more. Once

the girl had cleared the board and backed out, I stood up.

I said: "Why is M. Luynes debauching Mme la marquise's servants?"

"M. Luynes is Mme la marquise's nearest male relation. He has reasonable expectations of her succession. If Mme la marquise takes a second husband, he shall find himself disappointed, as shall his many and various creditors. M. le comte de Luynes is a fool and a poltroon but they are not. I would have thought, Mr Colonel, that you might have reasoned that."

"But, madame, if he is as worthless as you say, why should Mme de Maurepas favour him?"

"Mme de Maurepas has some pride of family. Really, Colonel, you were not always so slow. I advise you not to bank on her generosity."

With difficulty, I controlled myself. Then Mme de Bussy said: "Or are you become one of our famous Solognots, who feigns imbecility for his own profit, and gives six liards for two sols?"

The interview saddened me and put me out of temper. I asked myself: Must we all, as we age, decay in moral character? By what perverse intention had Mme de Bussy made sure I would not again visit her? And why will nobody in this fair land of France credit a disinterested sentiment?

Those questions were too large and long for my purposes. Instead, I attempted to see myself through the eyes of Mme de Bussy and the desert district. What was I but a penniless trooper who, by a scheme of surgery, not, in itself, hard to acquire, had gained an ascendancy over a sick woman? As for the orphan, had I not myself introduced her into Mme la marquise's good graces? For an instant, I lost my grasp on what is, and saw myself and my young friend in this criminal light. I pulled myself together. Now if Mme de Bussy sent word to M. Luynes of my inquiry, which I thought at least certain, was that not all to the good? Would it not oblige him, as we say at sea, to show his colours?

Lost in such thoughts, and some more sinister, I looked up to see a horseman coming at me between the pollards at a hand-gallop. I recognised M. Dalouhe, gave spur and we raced heel-to-heel to the castle. Before the bridge, we reined in and I sprang down while M. Dalouhe took away the winded horses.

In my lady's laboratory, the huntsmen seemed to have come in a body from the barber's and tailor's. I was myred with muck. Mme de Maurepas came in and sat down. Mme Nicolette stood at her shoulder.

M. Duclos proddled a young man forward. The lad opened his mouth and said:

"They are here. I mean, the same men. Both."

Mme de Maurepas shivered.

I was touched that M. Duclos had allowed the young man to bring the news. What a soldier was lost in this huntsman!

The lad had dried up. M. Duclos took up his tale:

"M. Viollet found them at Priors' Hill last night, and stayed in ambush while they bivouacked. He was relieved an hour ago. They are now moving southwards. They have not yet breakfasted."

"Thank you, M. Viollet. I shall not forget your service." Mme de Maurepas looked about her and settled, after a while, on me.

I could see through the window a puffle of smoke from the kitchen. I allowed my questions to subside like scalded milk. I had resigned command, for good reason, and must honour that.

"We must wait, if you can bear it, my lady, until dinnertime."

We waited and waited. I have known the hours before a pitched battle pass at a smarter tempo. Alert to any hint of reverie or inattention among his men, M. Duclos gave out small tasks, posed me questions of no great importance, spoke of natural history to Mme la marquise. All that time, he seemed to be listening to the sounds of the woods that were as familiar to him as to a wild beast.

M. Duclos stiffened.

At the kitchen door, I saw the foundling receiving, with a curtesie, a steaming basket.

Mme de Maurepas stood up.

"You are to halt at once and take the child to safety."

M. Duclos said nothing.

"Do you intend, M. Duclos, to disobey me?"

At length, the young man answered. "No, my lady. I shall call off the action and take responsibility for any misconsequences."

Whatever Mme de Maurepas had expected, it was not that. "I shall not intermeddle," she said. "You must do as you deem best."

We waited, listening.

From a distance, as if strained through miles of birch and wind, came the sound of a hunting horn and then, from further away, a second. M. Duclos made a sort of a bark and, remembering he was not among adepts, said: "We have the men. Mlle Marie-Ange is safe. Will you permit me to take my leave?"

I turned back from the window. "M. Duclos, may I inquire your usual conduct with the poaching men you apprehend?"

M. Duclos seemed to be asking himself how much he should say. "They spend the remainder of the night in the guard, Colonel, and then are brought to Her Ladyship."

"Shall you not conform to that procedure in this more serious case?"

A covered wagon, which I estimated to be in ordinary use to transport the hunt beaters, halted before the corps-de-garde. From its rear, two hooded men were brought down. I could see only their feet. Those were well shod. They were soldiers or invalids. I said to myself: Now, gentlemen, let us find your captain.

To the room at large, I said: "I would propose that the men have neither nourishment nor water. They are soldiers, and are accustomed to scant commons. In addition, my lady, will you kindly order that the servants' dinner be placed to cool on the parapet by the guard-house and that M. Dalouhe wash the carts and horses there?"

"That is torture, Mr Neilson."

"As you command, my lady."

"These wicked acts I shall bear on my conscience and mine alone. Do as Mr Neilson requests."

One of the lads brought in a packet. Unwrapped, it revealed two long knives. Mme de Maurepas had them laid beside her microscopium.

After a time, she said: "These knives have not been used. They are quite unmarked."

I sprang to the door but the lads easily beat me. I surrendered. I turned to Mme de Maurepas and said:

"Their breakfast. The men used knives to cut their meat and ate it on the thumb."

After some five minutes, M. Duclos and M. Dalouhe returned. Mme de Maurepas blenched. There was blood on their faces and hands, which they had done nothing to remove, and a crimson gash in M. Duclos's sleeve.

She said: "You have given blood in my service."

"A scratch," M. Dalouhe said, which it was.

"I shall now attend to the legalities of the men's imprisonment. M. Dalouhe, you are to send one of your men to ride at pace with my letter to M. le gouverneur."

I said: "Do not you yourself have rights of seigneurial justice, madame?"

"I do, Mr Neilson, but the Kings of France have over the years sought to abridge them. I do not know why. My power, alas, is not absolute."

Mme la marquise de Maurepas was herself again.

Through the window, I saw Dalouhe, reeking with gore, spring onto a stamping horse. The beast rose on its hind-legs. M. Dalouhe raised his hat to the house, then rattled over the bridge.

XXV

In reasoning, whether in abstract philosophy or a criminal affair, there are two principal methods of inquiry. We may, like Aristotle, range over the various phenomena so as to cast up a principle common to them all; or, in the manner of Sir Isaac Newton, lay down a principle known or proved from the beginning from whence we account for all the distinct and several appearances. This latter is the more philosophical method and more fit to hang the right man.

I knew that it was M. Luynes who had hired the old soldiers, as did M. Duclos, as did Mme la marquise de Maurepas. It was necessary to reason from that premiss, and carry Mme la marquise through every step of the reasoning so that there should not be a speck of doubt in her mind as to that gentleman's guilt.

I could not from my hollow purse myself journey to

Paris, or pay the hire of a courier. I might take myself to Orléans, to dice with officers at the Vache Noire, or hold up the post-coach on the Toulouse high road, but neither course would be greatly to my lady's honour. I consigned my letters to the ordinary. My credit at the Intendance of Troops was better than I had hoped. I received by return the strength of M. Luynes's company. Two of the names had been rayed or struck out, with the abbreviation for a dishonourable discharge. The names were still legible.

For all that, the villains were good soldiers. After two days, during which the men said nothing at all, Mme de Maurepas allowed them water lest they die. In conveying the lady's order to M. Duclos, I gave him my news from Paris. That evening, at the assembly, M. Duclos said:

"We have the names of the men. Jacques Carnot and Roland Benard."

"How do you know, M. Duclos?"

"It is better that I do not say."

Mme de Maurepas made as if to remonstrate, and then thought better of it.

"The men are in passable health, madame."

Mme de Maurepas said nothing.

"Do you have their places of regular or original abode, M. Duclos?"

A FOUNDLING

"Yes, Colonel."

"My lady, may I propose you send an emissary to their families?"

"The emissary will frighten them and cause them to shut up like mussel-shells."

Mme Nicolette spoke up.

"Will you permit me to go, madame? I will speak to their mothers, woman to woman."

After a moment, Mme de Maurepas said:

"Yes. You will have the coach-and-pair. Dalouhe will attend you on the box."

Mme Nicolette had, once again, killed two birds with one stone.

XXVI

Some four or five night had passed, when I was wakened by running feet and candles flashing through cracks and chinks. On the wet pavement below the window, I made out a strange horse held upright by two grooms, its back and flanks smoking.

"My lady, will you rise and dress? M. Dalouhe has returned."

I found the valiant man sprawl'd and spatter'd by the door, M. Duclos pouring water down his throat, but no Mme Nicolette. I put my finger to my lips.

Mme la marquise entered. She was in half-dress, a shawl over shoulders, her hair falling down, dark as a river after a storm. M. Dalouhe made as to rise, but M. Duclos pushed him down.

M. Duclos said: "Mme Marrin has found Benard's mother. They are following in the coach, Mme Marrin taking the reins."

M. Dalouhe caught his breath. "Mme Nicole says that if she has overstepped…"

Mme de Maurepas closed her eyes. She said, as to herself only: "Is there nothing that girl cannot achieve?"

M. Duclos and, if it were possible, M. Dalouhe sagged like pricked bladders. I had not known that they had established a monopoly of my lady's favour, and could not tolerate the commerce of an interloper.

Mme de Maurepas opened her eyes. "Gentlemen!" she said. "Are not we ladies to have a share of the battle honours?"

The lads pulled themselves together.

Mme de Maurepas said: "I ask myself if I should put

the respectable Mme Benard to such trouble. At any rate, I shall pass the interesting news to her son."

Mme la marquise turned to me. "Will you not, Mr Neilson, lend me for a moment your pistols? I do not think I shall discharge them."

"I shall light you."

"That will not be necessary. Kindly order refreshment for M. Dalouhe, who has done well, as have you, M. Duclos."

Placing the pistols in the guschet of her dress, one on each side, Mme de Maurepas walked to the door, which opened on a false dawn.

"Damn," I said, under breath; and then for the two men, "Patience, if you please."

M. Dalouhe looked robbed of his wits. On M. Duclos's face was a look of despair.

It was light by the time Mme de Maurepas returned. She took out the pistols and placed them on the hall table. There was no misting of the varnish. They were cold. She said:

"When you are fully recovered, M. Dalouhe, will you ride out and overtake the coach and take Mme Benard back to Rouen. She is not now required. I shall give you a present to take to her."

"And the assassins?" That was M. Duclos.

"I have ordered them some light nourishment. I have told the Captain of the Guard that the men may leave at first light, with provisions and a little journey-money. If they so much as take a step on my lands again, I shall with my own hand string them from the King's oak. They appeared to judge that fair."

There was not a word from M. Duclos.

"In return for your service in this ordeal, I have decided on a general promotion. The places of Master-of-Horse and Chief Huntsman of my properties have for some time been hereditable offices. I shall today buy back those charges. The annual wages, which were 800 francs and 950 francs, but which I shall equalise at 1,000 francs, you shall each have for your own just so long as you are in my service. Your men will receive gifts at your selection and discretion."

M. Duclos said: "I require no additional reward, madame. It is my duty as a man and a Christian to aid the orphan and the widow."

M. Dalouhe, who was spending in advance his fortune in presents for his mistress, woke from a fever of painted Indiennes and English lace. He said: "For myself, I need no wage at all. Just to serve such a generous lady is reward enough."

Mme de Maurepas stifled a cough.

"Forgive me. The damps of dawn in the province. My friends, I have enlarged your appointments not simply to reward you for your courage and loyalty." Mme la marquise was gasping at air. "I would have you found honest families, and cease to trouble the hearts of my girl-servants."

M. Dalouhe blushed. On M. Duclos's face, there was a look of introspection. Of his fidelity to Mme de Maurepas, I had not the smallest doubt. What troubled me was there seemed to be no limit to that fidelity.

After the lads had left, Mme de Maurepas said: "And you, Mr Neilson, will you not have something from me? A gold-mine, perhaps, or some populous trading city?"

"I have all that I need."

"Oh, Mr Neilson, if you will have from me neither riches nor honours, how can I govern you?"

"I have heard that some ladies ensure an efficient government by sometimes conferring and sometimes withholding their most particular favour."

"I could not do that. It would be unworthy. You either love or not love. There is no policy in it."

"I am glad, madame."

XXVII

It was a long day but darkness came, as she must. M. le comte de Luynes stood a moment in the lamp-light on the terrace. He was accustomed to being looked at. It was as if, to an imaginary public, he were saying: "In the soup again with old Aunt Moneybags. Really, I don't know which saint to pray to."

In reality, a dozen pairs of eyes were fixed upon his face, and as many loaded hunting-pieces.

I said to the window-glass: "I should have told you, sir, but Mme de Maurepas detests gayety in masculine dress."

"Little shite."

I turned. M. Duclos was standing in the shadow.

"We must take the impression of the horse shoe-irons."

He held up a hand. From below, I heard Mme Marrin.

". . . and disappoint the kitchen-maids. Come now, Mr Coachman, a cup of chocolate in the back-kitchen will do you no harm. And Dalouhe will wash His Lordship's coach."

"That shall I do with pleasure, my neighbour."

I heard the calash rumble over the bridge.

"You are to do nothing to M. Luynes. Do you understand, M. Duclos?"

"I am not aware, Mr Colonel, that I take orders from you."

"I did not give an order. If you assassinate M. le comte de Luynes, the crime will be laid at the door of Her Ladyship."

"She will let him go!"

"Remind me, if you will, who 'she' is."

M. Duclos blazed in anger and mortification. "I mean Mme la marquise."

"Please sit, M. Duclos." I walked two steps up and two steps down the tiny room.

"Do you want a drink, Colonel?"

"Yes."

He passed me a flask of some forest tonic.

"Colonel, I must have a decision. If that man has done this once, he will do it again. He would strip the wings from an angel."

"Another drink, if you please."

There was a whistle and another wormwood flask appeared, and with it M. Dalouhe's sketch of the shoe-iron. It was as expected, like the conclusion in logic or the last card turned up at pharaon. It was the particular craft mark of the farrier at Vaultrien, and the spit of the print in the sand.

I said: "You may do nothing that may, by her worst enemy, be imputed to the order or even wish of Her Ladyship. Tomorrow is Sunday. If you will be so kind, you will hold yourself ready to attend me on a short journey. With your side-arms. In your Sunday clothes. And M. Dalouhe, if he is not otherwise occupied."

XXVIII

It was not until near midnight that M. Luynes appeared on the terrace by torch-light. It could have been worse, he seemed to say to his phantom auditory, though not very much worse. As he was helped into his coach, a party of horsemen clattered over the bridge and formed escort.

I do not know what M. Duclos said, but the glasses went up with a crack. The coachman's coat was black with sweat. The conveyance wandered from side to side, as if driven by a happy drunkard, its lamp bobbing away until it could no more be seen.

I made my way to my lady's apartments, knocked and entered.

Mme de Maurepas was standing at her escritoire, a burner lit, sealing letters.

"Come in, dear friend," she said. "I have had an unexpected visitor, M. le comte de Luynes, my nephew. He has a mind to start anew in Louisiana. He asks for my interest with the governor at New Orléans, M. Vaudreuil." She looked at me. "Have I done well, Mr Neilson?"

"Yes, madame. For myself, I do not believe that M. Luynes will survive a quarter-hour in Louisiana."

"I am your inferior in some respects, Mr Neilson, but I know better than you our French nobility. There are men in that estate so delinquant that they can only come to life running through the American woods. Perhaps that vicious young man, good now only for the wheel and the rope, might yet do something for his country and his age."

"It is possible. Before that, and I mean this very Sunday, I shall ride over and give him my challenge."

"You shall not, Mr Neilson."

"I shall, Mme de Maurepas."

"Mr Neilson, if you swore a little less and prayed a little more, you would know that Our Lord will always forgive the contrite."

"Why should M. Luynes, of all people, be granted a second chance?"

"M. Luynes has had a second chance."

"Bloody hell and damnation."

"How dare you swear at me! Leave me at once."

"I shall do so, but first I would wish you to hear me. Your family pride and the clatter of the district mean more to you than the life of a young girl you profess to love more than—"

Mme de Maurepas hit me in the face. I fell back on my rocky ankles, threw out an arm and knocked a China vase into shivers.

"More than that, you knew from the beginning that it was he—"

"That is a disgusting lie!"

She rained blows on my face, while, with her knees and feet, attempted to demolish that part of me which she had of late been rather inclined than not to favour. My ankles buckied and I fell back into the bookcase, which with the force came off the wall, and engulfed me in folios and mahogany.

There was a shriek and Mlle Marie-Ange, in her nightgown, came running in on bare feet, swept something off the escritoire, and began to escalade the book-case. In her hand was a pen-knife. I pulled back my head and it buried into a volume. Enraged, she spat in my face.

"What are you doing, puppet? Where did you learn to do that?"

"At the Hospital."

"You must never, ever do that again. Please, my darling, leave me to deal with this man. That, you villain, is an abominable falsehood . . ."

"Madame, you rang." Mme Nicolette was in the doorway.

"I did not, Marrin."

It was too late. Mme Nicolette, thinking to see in my dripping cheeks some authority or precedent of her mistress, climbed two shelves and spat in my face.

"Marrin! What are you doing? Why are my servants spitting?"

"I knew from the beginning that he was after your property."

"The Colonel was not after my property. He was the only man in France who was not after my property. That is why I used to like him."

"Do not fear, madame, the guard will finish him off."

"No!" The foundling threw herself across me. It was not so much that she had changed sides, but rather she must always side with the weaker contingent. "You said you loved him!"

"I did love him. I do not any more. I shall dismiss him and then we shall be happy, you and I and Marrin." The orphan was squalling with tears. "Please, Marrin, take the child to her chamber and console her."

"Now, you wretch, where was I?"

"Abominable falsehood."

"Yes. That revolting calumny . . ."

There was a beating on the door.

"Who is that, now?"

"It is I, my lady, come in strength to rout your foes. May I request that you retire with your ladies into your cabinet, for there will be fire and shot? And, my lady, should I fall in the action, I would wish—"

"Lieutenant Foible! I am engaged in an important quarrel with Colonel Neilson. If you wish to serve me, you will leave me in peace for five minutes."

"We are ready at your call."

"Now, where was I?"

"Revolting calumny."

Mme de Maurepas was fashed, but not with me, who alone stood with her in upholding the ancient privilege of lovers to throw things at each other. The savagery of her allies disgusted her. She was rather as one of our officers in Canada, who, raiding into New England and helping the minister's wife out of the burning manse, turns and sees his Abénakise scout dash her babies' brains against the door-post.

"Mr Neilson, so that you know, I said *second chance* with a particular meaning. Some time ago, I paid M. de Luynes's table debts against his promise to give over all kind of play. That was the second chance he squandered."

Mme de Maurepas paused. "Mr Neilson, if I may say so, you look a little droll."

"I am sure I do, madame. I am sorry for the damage I have caused."

"Do not mind the vase. I have more of that ware. Rather too much, in effect. They were sent by Kubilai Khan to the eighteenth count. Three cases are still packed up in the commons. As for the books, they are works principally of theology and devotion that I had been used to read on retiring, before you introduced me to sinning."

"I do not know the sin of it, my lady."

"Really, Mr Neilson, are we to talk morals on such a night! Do you not see that I have settled my succession – my succession! – which gave the Parlements of France their bread and cheese for twenty years and built the fauxbourg Saint-Germain at Paris? Great property can be a burden, Mr Neilson, which sits like a weight upon the breast."

"I believe I know what you mean, madame."

"Now, shall you wait here while I console the child? I shall return, presently, with the preliminaries of peace."

To relieve my chest, I began to dislodge some of the volumes, and I may have failed a little in the respect due their ghostly authors. As I worked through the shelves, I saw that there was in the whole library not the smallest tint of unorthodoxy. Of Jansenius, there was not a sniff. In throwing down M. le cardinal de Noailles's *Pastoral Letter on the Bull Unigenitus,* I succeeded in moving my right leg.

I had opened and poured some Champagne when my lady, in négligée and her hair loose, returned. She said: "I propose a treaty which requires, from each of us, all but intolerable sacrifices but will give us space to breathe for a year or two. Will you sit while I expound it to you?"

"I shall stand."

"Please sit, Mr Neilson. There is no victor here, and no vanquished."

I sat down in an arm-chair.

"Now, in the first article, you consent not to challenge M. le comte de Luynes. For that reason, you will suffer the obloquy of having refused to defend your mistress. That you must suffer."

She stopped and looked at me.

"Why are you looking at me?"

"You are sitting."

"You insisted I sit."

"Yes. I like you sitting. It is more equal. Or nearly equal."

Mme de Maurepas continued: "It is many weeks' sailing to New Orléans. There are hazards of wind and sand and weather. I may not receive an answer from M. Vaudreuil for a year. If, when he writes, he tells me that M. Luynes is in the colony and serving the King, I ask that we do no more. If on the other hand, His Excellency writes that M. Luynes has not come to the colony or arrived but at once absconded to the English in Carolina or the Spanish at Havana and Mexico, I release you from your promise so you may fight him."

She took breath, then went on. "Secundo. I shall dispose of my property. Much the larger part shall pass by what we call a *donatio inter vivos*, or donation between living persons, to the found child named Marie-Ange de la Contrition whom I shall appoint my sole heiress and legatee. She shall be addressed as Mlle de Joyeuse. The smaller part I shall retain so that I can look after you. Further, if you will permit me, I shall accompany you oversea to find this man. If you succeed in killing M. Luynes by fair means, I shall ask you to let me care for you in a cabin on the Pascagoula or some such place, where we shall subsist by a harmless agriculture. Should you fall in combat, I shall by feminine deceit and treachery myself kill the comte de Luynes, and then submit to whatever system of justice or retribution obtains in that place. Now, Mr Neilson, is that fair?"

"Madame, I do not require you to avenge me."

"Hey-ho, Mr Neilson, must you always quibble about particulars! Do you not see that we have here the makings of an honourable life which, I may add, permits Mlle de Joyeuse the untroubled enjoyment of her estate?"

She looked about her ruined chamber. "Dear friend, I would have you mark that the property you destroy in your incessant quarrelling is no longer wholly mine to dispose. The next time you have a mind to insult me, shall we not seek out the open air?"

"A wise project, my lady."

She stood up. "There is an unforeseen vacancy of my bed. Should you wish to join me there, you are welcome. If you have further wishes, I would have you fulfil them in brusque, selfish and ungallant fashion, for I have no other desire tonight than for sleep."

XXIX

Beneath my window next morning was a coming and a going of carts and luggage. It seems that, along with everything else, M. Luynes had informed on his confederates in the house, and they were leaving the service of Mme de Maurepas. If he had hoped to frighten his aunt into sending me away, his stratagem had rebonded on him in the rout of his party. In side-stepping a puddle, he had fallen into a ditch.

It cannot have been a pleasant hour for M. Luynes, rolling those three or four leagues to the limits of his aunt's lands, while her huntsmen scraped their skinning-knives down the glasses; but a premonition, if he would mind it, of what he must expect across the water should he defraud or otherwise displease those irritable Americans, the Chickasas.

Yet there was something in it that I misliked. A bad subject he was, sure enough, M. Luynes, but a murderer of a young girl?

As the story of the quarrel went back and forth between the neighbouring houses, it became a sort of battle of giants or Gigantomachia in which I broke off crags and uprooted trees while Mme de Maurepas, crouched on the hearth-stone, hurled blazing firebrands at my head.

As Mme Marrin let fall a hint here and another there, like so many dropped handkerchiefs, a picture opened to view. A certain neighbour had offered insult to one of Her Ladyship's kitchen maidservants. Mr Neilson had sworn in fury to fight the villain. Mme la marquise had forbidden him on pain of dismissal. Such a conflict of masculine valour and feminine prudence was much to everybody's taste.

The Loyalists, who took their lines from Mme Marrin, became worldly. In a great affair of love (they said), all the passions grow strong, and anger and jealousy can burn like summer fires. The Frondeurs, too depleted to contradict, wondered, more in sorrow than anger, if the Parlement of Paris might not break a testament drawn up amid violence and at mid-night. Mme la Marquise, now she had seen the monster in her Scottish fancy-man, would dismiss him and who else, outside the stables or the kitchen, would take his rests and give her a legitimate heir. As for the kitchen slut, she would traipse the streets of Orléans as had her mother before her. M. Luynes would come into his own.

M. Ballin had saved his citizen's skin. How he had done so I neither knew nor sought to know. I suspect that Mme de Maurepas wished to have him under her eye. I did not think she had forgiven him.

Heroes of the hour, the huntsmen made asses of themselves. They took to parading with a badge on their surcoats whose meaning they would not divulge. They affected a languor of gait, softness of voice and mansuetude of gesture. They forswore the razour and the comb. In such an open-air existence, their pallid visages must have owed a muckle to chalk. Mme de Maurepas reported that they infested the Mass, limping to the rail with heads bowed and pressing the Easter Bread against trembling lips. Each evening, two of their number set out into the woods to beat the coverts for mishandled beggar-maids. I do not know if they found any, but they always returned under poles hanging with vermin.

That had an unforeseen consequence.

"What is that bird, madame?" We were lazing on her window-seat.

"It is a nightingale. They have not been here since I was a girl. They began singing last night."

"What is she saying?"

"He. He is saying: Come down, and perch near me,

my hen, and I will show you happiness of which my song is just a prelude or overture."

"And she says: Now I am here, I would have you sing with diminished ardour. And shall you not perch, sir, a little more the upright?"

"Are you teasing me?"

"Certainly, not."

An enchantment fell upon La Ferté-Joyeuse. Out on the terrace, men and women stood, immobile as statues, while the music wove into gauze about them. They shook their heads, took a pace, stopped, started again, stopped. Returning to my room, I found a smashed pane and a broken cross-bow bolt. Tied to the shaft was an order that I attend on a certain night at a certain place The Trial Most Sharp of Death and Rebirth.

I asked my lady's leave not to attend, but she insisted I go. Further, I was to note, with the greatest precision, every stage of the ceremonial.

So it was that, one warm evening of that nightingale April, I set off, unarmed, in my shirt, barefoot, hands bound, blind-folded and facing my horse's tail. I fell into a dream and did not notice for a while that somebody or something had my mount's reins, and the wood chittered with animal noises. Rough hands threw me down. The blind-fold was cut. I found myself in a clearing in the twilight, surrounded by creatures with the bodies of men, and the heads of fox, boar, wolf, badger and lynx.

A stag drew a knife across my bare chest and drew blood.

"Mac-Neil! Do you swear eternal fealty to the Order of the Trampled Primrose?"

"I do, so help me."

"To serve faithfully the poor, the weak and the fair?"

"I do, so help me."

"To keep the Order's secrets beyond the gate of Death?"

"I do, so help me."

"Arise, Earle Mac-Neil, knight veteran of our Order."

There followed certain administrative business more conveniently treated, it seemed to me, in committee. As far as I could understand from the beastly speech, I was not a true knight of the Order (for that would never do) but a sort of *preses* or senior, charged with resolving disputes over precedence and punishing infractions. I was not looking forward to the second capital of my office, for the penalty of the most trivial delict was death.

Thence we passed to a torch-lit shooting-match, where I did myself small honour, and then to an eating-feast and drinking-bout, where I did better. The beasts only had to call out their toasts and drain their horns to fall to the grass of the clearing, where they made a kind of *agger* or heap. At the end, there was just the stag (whom I took to be M. Duclos in *incognito*), smoking his pipe on a fallen oak-tree. I lowered the hammers on the boys' fowling-pieces, bowed to the stag, walked backwards to my browzing horse, and clip-clopped under starlight back to La Ferté, facing her ears and much pleased by the access to my strength.

XXX

I was summoned by Mme de Maurepas in plain morning.

"I am sworn, madame, by fatal oaths, to secrecy."

"Come now, Mr Neilson. You may tell me."

When I remained obstinate, Mme de Maurepas let fall that she had heard speak of shaded ways in the garden of love that we might, with halting steps, follow to their ends. When that, too, failed to unhook my jaw, Mme la marquise changed her tack and declared that I was deceived to think that the rite preserved even a tint of druidical practice. It was but a giddy boys' game that it ill behoved an officer of the King, and a man in his fifth decade, to decorate with his presence. That was no more successful and we parted in sulks.

At noon, weary of Greek, I stood at my window. Mme Porcher lounged with her gossips on the bridge. A servant girl approached them from the house and, with a curtesie, passed between them. Head lowered, with slow step, she approached the huntsmen's lair. The farmwives hissed and chuttered.

"Now," I said out loud, "is the moment of the Order of the Trampled Primrose."

I need not have freted. The door opened and the men filed out. They formed a double hedge, fire-locks lowered, heads bare. Mlle Marie-Ange stepped between the lines. M. Duclos stood in the door and then descended to the ground. He handed the visitor up the double-step. The men followed in the order in which they had come out. The door closed.

Mlle Marie-Ange was indoors something under a minute. The manoeuvre was repeated in reverse. Mme Porcher stood, hands on hips, a feminine Horatius on the Sublician bridge. From the set of her mouth, she was saying to herself: I'll have the slut sent back to the Hospital where she belongs.

I pulled at the window but the catch came away in my hand. In agony, I watched Mlle Marie-Ange, with an incline of her head, step onto the bridge. Something in the child's dress or gait immobilised Mme Porcher, who turned to let her pass. Mlle Marie-Ange crossed the terrace to the main door, which snapped open to admit her. Mme Porcher had, by a whisker, saved herself no little inconvenience.

At two, Mlle Marie-Ange brought me my dinner. She set down the trey and looked away.

"I am to beg your pardon for assassinating you. And for spitting."

"I do not wish you to do so. If you thought Her Ladyship in danger, you did the right and the brave thing. Come now, young miss, shall we forget all that? How is your reading?"

"Tomorrow we start on Z, the most bizzzarre of the Greek letters, and the lazzzt of all the alphabet."

"Why are you sad, young miss?"

"I see that man in my dreams."

I had an inspiration.

"Would you like to learn to fight with the sword? Then, if that man haunts you in your dreams, you can send him flying. To recover my military fitness before I go into

Italy, I have engaged a master-of-arms at Orléans to come here for a week. It is small matter to that gentleman if he has a second, and more promising, pupil. What say you to that, young miss?"

I turned and found the lass was gone.

A little later, Mme de Maurepas stood outside my doorway, dressed to the nines.

"I cannot enter your room, Mr Neilson, because of my dress. May we converse standing?"

"Of course, my lady."

"Do not lean like that, Mr Neilson. You are not at the door of an inn."

"Evidently, my lady."

"I am ravished that Mlle de Joyeuse is to be instructed in the escrime."

Mlle Marie-Ange was signalling to me from behind her god-mother's shoulder.

"Stop that, you two!" Mme de Maurepas reached behind her and pulled the child to her front. "I will not be the only person in this house with any sense! How is it, Mr Neilson, that you, who has risen high in the King's service and surely one day, if I have anything to do with it, will have your general's baton; how is it, I say, that you behave with all the wisdom of an apprentice on Sunday eve?"

Mme la marquise de Maurepas, you cannot bring up this sad child on your own. Not Latin, Greek or the calculus, no, not all your god-motherly love, will chase away her fears or still her anger.

"I thought that perhaps..."

"Have you ever had a thought, Mr Neilson?"

"Yes. Several. Some. No."

"Don't be angry with the Colonel! It was my idea." Mlle Marie-Ange buried her head in Mme la marquise's skirts.

"I am not angry. I am never angry and certainly not with you, my darling. The Joyeuse women have ever known how to fight. I myself can load and discharge a pistol as well as any lady, or a little better. What I wish to know, Mr Neilson, is how, in your sword-fighting, you design to protect Mlle de Joyeuse from injury and calumny?"

"She shall use the foil, with a bouton on the tip and a milled blade. She shall wear a quilted plastron and safety-glasses such as you use in your laboratory. I shall be present at every bout, and examine the weapons after each pass."

"And her modesty?"

"My lady, that is a matter on which I have no expertise."

Mme de Maurepas turned away. "Granted on condition," she said.

XXXI

That night I received a visitor.

"May I sleep in your bed, Mr Neilson? Marrin and the child are in occupation of mine."

"Of course, I have long wished to return your nocturnal hospitality."

"Mr Neilson, do you know how to undress a lady?"

"No."

"Would you like to learn?"

"Yes."

"I shall now turn my back on you. Do you see two pleats hanging from the shoulders?"

"Yes."

"You may detach the pleats from the back."

"Done!"

"Now, remove the open robe, taking care to pick out any pins and not leave any hooks still latched.

"Now unlace the bodice at the back, detach the stomacher and lay them on one side."

"There! The whole top is done."

"You are but at the beginning, Mr Neilson."

Mme de Maurepas turned about. I was having difficulty staying to my task.

"Am I to unbutton this petty-cote thing?"

"Yes."

"But there's another! Of a different colour and stuff. And another, this time of a shade of rose or pink."

"Oh, Mr Neilson, the petty cotes are much of a muchness."

"What is this contraption?"

"It is my panier. To make the skirt larger in the round."

"Why?"

"Who knows? To make us ladies too large to ignore, or too slow to escape."

"I did not know that a lady's dress required such engineering."

"Yet, it is so. Now give me your hand so I can step out of my prison."

"Lord above! What is that?"

"There is no cause to swear at my underlinen, Mr Neilson. It is a chemise."

"Will you give it to me?"

"No."

"What is it for?"

"I believe for warmth, in part, and, in part, for modesty. Will you take it off me?"

"I shall try."

I succeeded.

"Ah! Stockings. I know about those. But what are those things at the top?"

"They are called jarretières. They hold the stockings in place."

"May I have them to keep?"

"No. You must unhook them."

That was easier said than done.

"Would you kindly turn about, my lady?"

Mme de Maurepas revolved.

"If I may say so, Mr Neilson, you are not doing very well. Why not leave the stockings and jarretières in their places? You have, I believe, most of what you need."

"What about your ankles?"

"Mr Neilson! Can you not defer my ankles!"

Mme de Maurepas stood in her stockings before me, like Eve after the dessert.

"So, Mr Neilson, now you have unwrapped your parcel, what do you intend to do with its contents?"

"Would you like to choose?"

"Yes. But you will have to lie down and close your eyes."

"Both of them?"

"Both of them."

After a time, Mme de Maurepas said: "Sometimes,

beloved man, I feel I am flying through the air. Do you feel that?"

"Not exactly."

"What do you feel?"

"I feel my heart will stop and my head burst."

"I see. I had better return to earth. Kiss me, if you wish, and hold me tight, so that in my descent I come to no harm."

We rested on solid ground.

"Mr Neilson, if you will permit me, I find that your bed is rather small?"

"It is perhaps not suitable to entertaining visitors. You shall have it for your sole possession and I shall do very well in the chair."

I looked about. The room was filled from floor to soffit in a snow of feminine undergarments.

"I had a chair, my lady, but I cannot now find it. And a window, too."

"Obstinate man, why will you not take my late father's apartments! But of course," she said, "the window! So you can command the approaches to the house. Oh Mr Neilson, did ever woman have such a strategist for defender?"

"Mme de Maurepas, you must recover your bed. It

is like the island battery at Louisbourg. Without it, we are lost."

"Come now, Mr Neilson. There is in the vertical plane somewhat more space than in the horizontal. I shall lie atop of you. Mind that you do not suffocate, for I need you tomorrow to value my English securities. As for me," she said, "I shall wake myself at midnight so that I may exult in my triumph. I have achieved what the Duke of Cumberland could not. I have vanquished a Neilson."

XXXII

Myron, the old footman, came stumbling through, followed by Mlle Marie-Ange, lunging at him with her foil. Her cotton armour and eye-glasses gave her a fearsome aspect.

"*En garde, maman!*"

Mme de Maurepas parried the blow with her quill. She said: "Can you not fight with the Colonel, puppet? The sword is his profession. Mine is the pen. And I am not your maman. I am your Latin teacher."

Mlle Marie-Ange turned and leaned on the button of her foil. She regained her breath. She said: "And so, vile

Colonel, at the breaking of the age, we are at last to meet."

"Aye, youth, and the rancounter is like to be fatal to one or t'other of us. Such insults bespeak no quarter..."

"...nor do such crimes!"

The lass was fast, but had not yet learned to disguise her intentions, and though I had but my officer's baton, which was a foot shorter than the foil, I could parry her blows. Her costume, which seemed at first to be a skirt, was split into two pantalons of the kind the Turkish ladies wear. In a week, or two at a stretch, she would be past me.

She stepped back and raised her hand-protector to her chin. She said: "You have had some instruction with the blade, Colonel. Yet your advancing years, your dissolute style of life, your disgraceful wounds and the burden of your crimes..."

"An old dog can still bite, fair youth. *Mettez-vous en garde!*"

Up and down we went, onto chairs and tables, along the book-shelves, behind the curtains, under tables, into and out of corners, over her god-mother's escritoire. Fearing for the porcelaines, I tripped and let the lass pin me to the panling by the fireplace.

Mlle Marie-Ange said: "It is for you, Mme la marquise de Maurepas, to pronounce the truant's doom. Shall you banish him to some desert fane where, in tears and sighs, he shall repent his crimes; or shall I send his soul a-fluttering down to Hell?"

"No fluttering! If you please, no fluttering!"

"Too late!" Marie-Ange pressed the fleuret against my throat. I tumbled to the carpet.

Somebody rapped and entered. It was Mme Nicolette. She shrieked. "Why is the Colonel lying on the floor?"

Marie-Ange glanced away. "*Vixit*. He has done his living," she said. "Yet in this hour of triumph, I can taste no joy. Dear friends, within this bloody wreck was once a youth, striding bright-eyed through the purple heath atop Squourr-na-Lapaique, or piloting his squiff between the wind-rumpled Orcades. A stranger to sin . . ."

"Marrin is here to make you ready for bed, puppet. Will you not abridge your oration?"

Mlle Marie-Ange stirred from her reverie. "*Manibus date lilia plenis*. Bring lillies in armfuls. Bear him up, my friends, and bury him by the roadside there, where the almond-tree above the wall shall every spring drape on his earth her winding-sheet of white." Head bowed, and sword lowered, Mlle Marie-Ange took Mme Marrin's hand.

For a while, I heard nothing but the scribble of Mme la marquise's pen.

"Don't you care to rise from the floor, Mr Neilson?"

"I am admiring your feet."

"Do you prefer them in slippers? Like this? Or like this, without?"

"I think, on balance, without."

"Mr Neilson, you choose the oddest parts of me to admire. You are like a well-bred visitor who, finding nothing to say about the pictures, raves about the sideboards."

"Mme de Maurepas, had I uttered such a sentence, you would have chided me for vulgarity."

"From you, it would have been vulgar. From me, not so. Why will you never sup with me, Mr Neilson?"

"Because we tiff, and then sulk in our own chambers, when we might be happy together. It is better that I come to you at ten for your blessing."

"We only tiff, as you are pleased to call it, Mr Neilson, because you provoke me beyond endurance. I suppose it is good military practice to be for ever probing your enemy. I do not inaugurate quarrels with you."

"No, my lady. And you are not my enemy."

"But you are mine. Each day, I must give another inch of ground to you. Not because you are more capable than I am, nor more clever, but because you are better.

I did not know that Scotland was such a nursery of virtue. Nor, so that you know, did I ask my darling to use that word. I would for all my life ransack the streets for her poor mother and reunite them."

"That is what the child wishes to call you, madame."

"It breaks my heart."

"I am sorry, madame."

Fearing I might petrify, I rose. I said:

"I had a dream last night when I was with you. Will you do me the greatest favour and write for me a letter?"

"Of course."

"May I say what needs to be said and then you shall put it in order? It is to Captain Harris, at Hanover-Square, London. If you will permit it, I propose you write in City of London cant. Because of the General Post Office spies."

Mme de Maurepas frowned but took up her quill.

"'Sir,

"'Your sample has arrived, somewhat damaged in passage, but in a generally satisfactory condition.'"

"Is that not for me to judge, Mr Neilson?"

"Yes, madame."

Mme de Maurepas was enjoying herself.

"'Thank you for the trouble you have taken with the merchandise. I hope that with the peace I shall be able to thank you in person. Would you write, at your earliest convenience, about the affair of Dorking?'"

"What, Mr Neilson, if you please, is dorking? I suppose it is some boisterous English rural sport."

"I believe it is a town or village in England, where dwells the young lady Captain Harris wishes to marry."

"Mr Neilson, you are all sentiment."

"'I am, sir, *et cetera*, J. Maurepas.'"

She laid her quill on the stand. She said: "I shall send it under cover to M. Martin, banker of Geneva. He will read it, of course, but that will do no harm. Indeed, the suspicion that I have commerce in London will make him all the more eager to serve me." Then: "Are you certain, Mr Neilson, that the dream came through the Gate of Horn?"

"I heard a voice on the battlefield in Scotland. H.R.H. the Duke of Cumberland was on horse-back above me. He said: 'Do your duty, God damn you, Mr Harris!'"

"But your Captain Harris did not do his duty. Or rather, he did."

Captain Edmund Harris had taken me prisoner in the late war in India. In the course of a most agreable captivity, we had become the best of friends; but, until I saw

Mr Harris in that dream of the battlefield, I would not have imagined he would risk his life to save mine.

The shame that had clogged my memory, like an alder fallen across a stream, the vision had dislodged and all manner of debriss came washing through my head. A certain M. Douvry, filibustier of Dunkirk, a man of elastic loyalties and inflexible price-tables, had carried me into Scotland on the eve of the battle. I could only presume that he had brought me off again, on credit. But how should M. Douvry recover his costs and a reasonable profit? I never had any money; and to hope for compensation from His Christian Majesty was a vain fantasy. I owed a debt of love to Mr Harris; but to M. Douvry I owed a very great sum of money.

XXXIII

The next morning, the weather being fine, I proposed to Mme la marquise de Maurepas that we ride out together. I wished to augment her confidence in her face and let her people see her and, just as important, see me.

She was reluctant. With the horses saddled at the

door, she pleaded headache, but the sound of my spurs on the stair must have put the bogles on her and she came out of her chamber in her riding clothes. Her palfrey was well-enough schooled, but she was not a born horsewoman, and her side saddell and slipper irons did not add to her mastery. Our progress was slow and not especially convivial. We stopped earlier than I had intended, where I made a fire and, for the second time in my life, made her a cup of chocolate. Mme de Maurepas had something on her mind.

At last, Mme la marquise said: "M. l'abbé Bignon has asked me to journey to Paris to deliver a discourse to the Royal Academy of Sciences on the inoculation against the small-pox."

"I had half-expected that, my lady, and have prepared for you some materials from the old Persian and Arab authors in your library."

"M. Bignon prefers the word *vaccination*. From the Latin *vacca vaccae*, meaning cow or large bovine."

"A happy coinage, madame. Have you been much in correspondence with the learned abbot?"

"After you left the île de France and went to India, I was dull. My lord had small use for me and I diverted myself with trifling researches. The abbé was kind enough to publish in the Academy proceedings my *Discourse upon the flightless birds of the Mascarenian Islands*."

And?

"Also *Some observations on the passive voices of the Malagasy tongue*. And some other things. So you see, Colonel Neilson, that I am that most detestable of creatures, a woman who dabbles in philosophy."

"If I had a wish, madame, it is that you should go to Paris. The King needs his best people, and the first woman is of more use to him than the last man. If she wishes to take coach, I shall attend her on horseback to the barrier and then take a turn in the country about. She has only to send for me when she designs to return."

"I shall not go. I seek only repose."

"Will you come a little way with me? I wish to show you something. Our horses will browze here."

We walked up a small eminence which gave a prospect of the surrounding country.

"May I hold your hand, Mr Neilson? Then, if your discourse is wearisome, I shall at least have the pleasure of your touch."

I launched my rivel-ravel. I said: "On my rambles, I have often come to this place and wondered if you might not consider some improvement. As you know much better than I do, the bottom lands are often inundated by the Sauldre and will bear no crop, while at the top, corn and timber spoil and beasts sicken for want of any transportation to market."

Mme de Maurepas relinquished my hand.

"Your thoughts, Mr Neilson, come only at rare and cherished intervals, like the prophecies of the Pythian priestess at Delphi. They should be heard with the strictest attention."

My project was not proceeding as I would have wished. I droned on:

"In the whole country, there are no coals, metals or lime, but a single mill in twenty miles, and scarce a tenant-farm that can pay three hundred livres in rent. Beneath the sandy loam, at a depth sometimes of just one or two feet, is a pann of slate on which the rains of winter lie in sheets but which dries to dust in summer. The people harvest just two or three times the rye they sow. There is no hemp for clothes and no milk for children and invalids. It occurred to me that the excavation of a canal might address such deficiencies, in both draining the low ground for corn and pasture and opening a sort of watery waggonway to the more distant settlements. The neighbouring ponds will serve as reservoirs for the canal in the dry season. Those slopes yonder that face south, with a gravelly soil, nourished vines in ancient times and should do so again."

"Are you finished, Mr Neilson?"

"Yes, madame."

"Colonel Neilson, when I instruct you in battles and sieges, then you may advise me on my property. And to make my little waterway, how much am I to pay?"

"Five hundred livres tournois per toise."

"Five million francs! What makes you think I have that in ready money?"

"Not all that shall be required at a time. I imagine that the heaviest or maximum requirement at any one time will be three millions. That you shall borrow on mortgage. It is too much for the capital market of Paris, but with your commission, and my known connexion with the late Mr Law, I shall pass by Amsterdam, Hamburg and Geneva."

"And where shall I find service to dig your canal? Or tenants to work your improved lands?"

"I believe, my lady, that the King would be happy to put the Champagne regiment now at Orléans at your disposition: provided, naturally, you take over its pay and provisioning."

"Pouf!"

"As for tenants, you may despatch me to recruit honest

and industrious farmers in the Palatinate and the Swiss Cantons."

"You shall settle no Protestants on my lands, Colonel Neilson."

"As you command."

"And how do you imagine these poor people will pay your canal tolls?"

"The canal will charge no toll. Navigation shall be free and gratis."

"Gratis! I now understand, Mr Neilson, how you come to be so poor."

I let that go by me. I said: "Your benefice, my lady, will arise in the augmentation of the value of the estate. Your lands will go from seven years' purchase—"

"Ten years."

"... to thirty years' purchase—"

"Twenty years."

"You shall be the richest subject in Europe, and the most beloved."

"I care for neither. Refused."

"The Sologne will be as happy as when King François and Queen Claude were at Romorantin."

"You are fatiguing me, Mr Neilson."

Having travelled so far, I resolved to go farther.

"This kingdom, madame, will not last for ever."

"I shall hear no sedition, Mr Neilson."

"Madame, I have seen the ruins of Isfahan and the empire of the Great Moghol sicken and crumple. Your posterity may not be as beloved as you are. Should matters go ill, the people will remember you and what you did for the poor people of the Sologne."

"What do I care for posterity?"

"Madame, did I not love you, I would not care for you."

"Likewise."

We walked in silence to our champing horses. Mme de Maurepas bent forward and fidged with my stirrup-straps.

"Colonel William, I am a woman who can do but one thing at a time. I am able to be happy and I am able to ride my horse, but cannot maintain, as it were, the two states of being simultaneously."

I had an idea. I knotted the reins of her horse, mounted my own and lifted Mme la marquise, side-on, in front of me.

I own that was dangerous and that I was dicing with her life, but I believed her horse would not interfere us, and the beast ran like a Christian, matching us pace-for-pace through the whistling birches, and all the while I held the most delicious armful any man could desire.

We passed foot-passengers, their open mouths but a flash of teeth. I saw that God had given us our portion of happiness not when we asked for it but when it could do us the best good.

When the towers of the castle appeared above the trees, I reined in, set Mme la marquise on the grass, and walked the horses in a circuit to cauld them down. Then we plodded home, my lady dozing on her side-saddle, I leading the horses, four faithful subjects of the King of France.

In the outer court, as the palfreyers scuttled towards her, Mme de Maurepas said: "Colonel Neilson, will you have the good nature this evening to sup with me in my small dining-room at eight o'clock. You need not dress. If you wish to flatter me, you may dab a little of the dust from your handsome cheeks."

At supper, I wore my order, but the ribbon was none too clean and the star prickled my breast. Mme de Maurepas was in dress, her hair piled high and millions sparkling from her hair and throat and bare bosom. Footmen stood in force against the panling of the walls.

"You are silent this evening, Mr Neilson. I have been better amused at the convent."

My eyes must have flickered to the footmen, for she smiled at me with malice.

"Sometimes, when we are alone, dear friend, you address me with certain words that I do not understand and I would wish translated into French or polite English."

"They are rustic endearments current in Scotland at the time of my youth. I do not know their translation."

"What? Such as 'Dear Lady' or 'Lovely Nymph'?"

"Not exactly so fine."

I must have stuttered, for Mme la marquise brought up reinforcements. "Also, sometimes in your dreams you cry out names. Who, if I may be so bold as to inquire, is 'Mollie' and 'Lennane' and the like . . . ?"

The face before me turned white as paper. Tears jumped from the eyes. She cried:

"Dismissed! All dismissed!"

The servants ran out.

"They are the Irish soldiers, madame, that, through a false manoeuvre, I did to death on Culloden Moor. They come to me in my dreams and rebuke me."

"Please take my hand, friend, if you can bear to. You would have thought that after so many years I might have gained an ounce of sense."

"I am frightened of dying, madame. They are waiting for me."

"They are, Mr Neilson. I thought they would resent

me for keeping you from them, but when a candle falls it snuffs before it touches the drugget, or when I slip on a greasy step, a hand steadies me and sets me upright. When all this comes to an end, which God in His mercy postpone, and you stand on the brink, you will hear such a cheer such as never was heard in Elysium and the banners will unfurl and the pipes play and the drums beat in joy that their great Captain has returned to them.

"Dearest friend, I invited you here tonight not to torment you but to honour you. I wished to show you that, though I am not beautiful, I might be elegant. I shall never again tease you, for I have no wit.

"Now, a gentleman at Venice, whom I do not know, M. Blondeau, who is consul and chief merchant of France in that Republic, sends me opera airs in the season and key-board music. I do not know why he sends such things and, when I return a bill in settlement, he does not encash it. I received from him this morning a toccata, which I would like you to show me how to play. Will you attend me in my music-room? I must make some restorations to my poor face."

Mme de Maurepas was good enough to lend me the Stainer violin, which needed nothing from me, and that was fortunate, for she played at her spinet, as they say in

Italy, "at first sight" and very fast. Then we danced together as at Port-Louis, the Stainer at my chin, while the footmen ranged against the wall gazed without seeing. Those exercises spared us gabbing, which was all to the good.

I woke to candle-light. Mme de Maurepas was standing before me, without a stitch on her, but a book in her right hand.

"Sleeping on watch, Colonel! And I the Duke of Cumberland's scout!"

"Few scouts look like Venus on her birthday."

"Kindly make room in my bed, which I remind you is my bed; stop staring at my waist; and read from holy writ. The twentieth chapter of St John. Start where you please."

"'And they say unto her, Woman, why weepest thou? She saith unto them, Because they have taken away my Lord and I know not where they have laid him. And when she had thus said, she turned herself back, and saw Jesus standing, and knew not that it was Jesus.' My lady, I cannot read this."

"Why not?"

"I am not worthy."

"You do not have to bear your sorrow, William. Our Lord shall bear it for you. You have but to ask Him."

"I shall bear it."

"As you please."

"I do not intend to return to the King's service."

"Mr Neilson, that is desertion. Who shall defend the poor and weak in this Kingdom, the orphan and the widow?"

"I have served the King of France for twenty-seven years. In that time, I have not received from His Majesty a dead liard. If ever you cease to require me as a servant, I shall take to the roads. I have a mind to go eastwards, to see the states of Germany and Austria, and Poland and Hungary, and Courland, and the frozen lands to the north."

"But how, my friend, shall you subsist?"

"By beggary, principally. I do not say, my lady, that if I pass a field of wheat in the ear, or a baker's cart stands unattended at the door of the inn, or a fat hen strays onto the highway, or a stallholder in the market of Breslau is distracted by a pretty woman, I shall not supplement what I receive in alms by some petty theft."

"Mr Colonel, will you permit me to accompany you on your tramp? I shall walk some paces behind you, so as not to trouble you with chatter or complaint. Though not pretty, I have a good shape, and you yourself have praised my bosom. I can play your decoy on market days."

"It will be a hard life, my lady, and not a long one."

"For God's love, Mr Neilson, will you let me follow you?"

"Yes."

XXXIV

Our honeymoon lasted four month. It ended not by reason of familiarity, for we were still as foot-passengers jossling in a foggy vennel, but for a clay tobacco-pipe.

Each morning, at seven, Mme la marquise de Maurepas attended Mass in the chapel in the north-eastern tower of La Ferté-Joyeuse. During that time, it was my habit in fine weather to sit on a seat on the terrace, and smoke a pipe of tobacco. During this fifteen or twenty minutes, Mlle de Joyeuse brought me a cup of coffee she was kind enough to make after the Turkish fashion with her own hand, and a glass of iced-water.

One pretty morning in the first week of May, 1747, I was enjoying those treats, which were not without some profane ceremony. My eyes were closed against the sunshine.

A shadow passed and then repassed. Mme de Maurepas stood before me, in a broad straw hat over her face and full dress, Mme Marrin and M. Ballin in attendance. I stood up.

"May I inquire what you are doing, sir?"

"It is called the tobacco, a pleasure I discovered in India."

"You shall stop this instant!"

I broke the hot pipe in my palm.

Her eye alighted on the tray with its saucer and glass. "I see he now gives orders to my servants."

"He does not, and has never done so. He has heard somewhere that faithful servants anticipate their mistresses' wishes."

Mme de Maurepas blazed. "Leave me a moment with this gentleman," she said.

That was not necessary. Mme Nicolette and M. Ballin were running for the house. From the kitchen range, I heard the slam of bars and shutters.

"Now, sir," Mme de Maurepas said with malice. "Will you take a turn with me in my garden?"

"With the greatest pleasure."

I took her arm but she shook me away.

"I have long wished to direct your attention to aspects

of your conduct which are not worthy of you, and cause pain to your friends."

"I shall be glad of instruction as to how to remedy them."

"I will not speak of your failings of good manners, which are but to be expected of a Scottish man bred in the shop and the camp. I leave apart your smoking, gaming and horrid swearing, your dishevelled dress, vulgar discourse and familiar conduct with my under-servants, your improvidence and irremediable frivolity. I mean this. In all the time I have known you, you have made not a single display of Catholicity."

"Mme la marquise forgets that I buried François Delacour in God's ground when every Catholic in the île de France but she was happy to leave him to the dogs."

"You are a captious man, along with your other faults. I meant that you did not attend Mass even at the Feast of Easter. Am I to conclude that you are a Turque or a Hindou or an adherent of the Pretended Reformed Religion?"

"Mme de Maurepas may conclude as she reasons. I ask leave to say just this. To attend Mass, I must first confess my sins and mend my sinful ways. During that time of penitence, I could not attend Mme la marquise to the extent that I desire and she merits."

Mme la marquise de Maurepas turned and ran back

under the limes. I felt sick at my unkindness. Why had I fallen into religion? Of all the things of which I know nothing? Of all things the most precious to Mme de Maurepas? My ankles pained me. I hobbled up to my room, where I wrote the following letter:

I have business in Italy. I have postponed the journey for fear of displeasing Mme la marquise. Now I have displeased her, I believe my absence for eight or ten weeks may not be unwelcome to her. I hope from my heart that I will find her, on my return, inclined to forgive her wretch of a servant Neilson.

The letter procured an immediate summons.

I had expected a renewal of the storm. I found, on the contrary, that Mme la marquise de Maurepas had become soft and winning.

"Please sit down, dear friend."

I remained standing, and Mme de Maurepas did not insist.

She said: "I regret my shrewish behaviour this morning, but it was not without cause. You may recollect, Col. Neilson, that you were bold enough to make a request for my hand."

"From my despair, I make it again."

"It is for that reason, and that alone, that I inquired into your religion."

I was sure that was not true. It had, as it were, by her saying it now, become true.

She lowered her head and said: "May I ask you the favour of delaying your journey into Italy? As you know, I intend to adopt Mlle Marie-Ange as my daughter and heiress. To do so, while at the same time you leave the house, would make the falsest of false impressions."

I sensed that even she found that feeble justification.

"I have made a promise and I must try to fulfil it."

"You have made promises to me. Or do they count for less?"

"I swear that, of my old life, this is the last entanglement. Once it is discharged, I will return and serve only you. Oh, don't weep, Jeannette..."

"I am not weeping. And my name is not Jeannette. I am not a market-wife."

I said: "At the wreck of the *Prince-de-Conty*, I promised a shipmate that I would deliver an object of value to King James of England, Ireland and Scotland. That man, an Irish priest of the seminary at Nantes, and a secret agent of the Stuart Court, perished in the wreck and so could not discharge me of this burden that I have borne with pain ever since."

"Do not go to Rome. That spider will draw you into his web and we shall lose you."

"You shall never lose me."

"Would it help you if I knew the character of this object?"

I drew out the jewel and placed it on the table at her feet. Mme de Maurepas glanced at it and looked away.

I said: "It is a diamond of perfect water and a weight of 490 carats. I am told it is worth two millions of sterling—"

". . . and it will rig out thirty ships and send twenty thousand soldiers to die in the heather, like your poor Irish men, and this time you will die with them. And what for? The English love to chase their kings. They change them as ladies change their stockings. They will never invite that family back. Do not carry that hellish thing to Rome. Take it out and cast it into the deepest lake in the district and never think of it again."

"I must fulfil my promise to a dying man."

Mme de Maurepas stood up. She said: "Only you can see your duty, Colonel Neilson. There was another reason for which I detained you, but I shall not now broach that.

Go with my blessing and in the protection of Our Lord and His Blessed Mother."

She held out her hand for me to kiss.

"I shall return and never leave."

"I do not think you shall. You shall die in Scotland and I shall live as many weary years without you as I have lived up to now. Sometimes I do not know what God wishes from me."

Mme de Maurepas shook off her humour. She said: "You would oblige me if you would write sometimes from Italy to Mlle de Joyeuse, who loves you even when she tries to assassinate you. Will you now kindly come with me? I wish to show you something to your advantage."

Ah, I thought. Sable, ane cover'd chalise argent.

"My lady, I am not worthy."

Mme de Maurepas turned and smiled. "Who are you to say, William, if you are worthy or not worthy? Am I worthy? Is the foundling worthy?" She took from a guschet in her robe an iron key. She said: "Stay with me a moment, William, and then leave, without saying goodbye."

We walked the gallery as far as the chapel but, instead of climbing up to it, dropped a step to a low door. Mme de Maurepas opened it. I followed her into a small room with a vaulted ceiling and lit not by a window but from a pair of candles on an oak board. Between them was a dish of glass, banded with simple strips of gold wire, and so broken it appeared not clear as glass but white as snow.

To my unlettered eye, the dish looked to be Iranian work, made at Nishapour or Rhey in the last years before Arab dominion, but mere antiquity was not the reason Hugues de Joyeuse had paid a king's ransom at Antioch to possess it. He believed it to be the Saint Graal in which Our Lord took his last meat on earth and which caught the dripping blood from His wounded side. It was the palladium of his house, its guarantee and its succession. The bowl had not fallen and broken on the pavement but been shattered with hammers or swords. It had been smashed beyond repair, and yet it had been repaired. It contained what was broken and mis-shapen in the world, all failure, shame and sorrow, put back together in countless hours of labour as an image of that world beyond where all is made whole again. I knelt beside Mme de Maurepas. After some minutes, I left without saying goodbye.

At the door, Mme Nicolette was holding my gaberdine and my hat.

"Why is Her Ladyship upset, Mme Nicolette?"

"If she don't tell you, nor do I."

Then she said: "M. Pierre has cleaned and charged your pistols. He has also made some things for you as protection on the road."

She dissolved in tears.

"What is it, Mme Nicolette?"

"He wishes to accompany you."

"What does Her Ladyship say?"

"She says only you alone can devise your plan of campaign."

"What do you say, Mme Nicolette?"

"I say the same. Please come back, Mr Colonel, for we are dull without you."

M. Pierre had my horse at the base of the steps, and also another, loaded to the elbows with arms and provisions.

"You are a good soldier, Pierre Dalouhe. Your duty, in my absence, is to protect the ladies and the orphan. Do you understand, M. Dalouhe?"

"Yes, Colonel."

I kicked down the avenue.

PART 2

Under the Leads

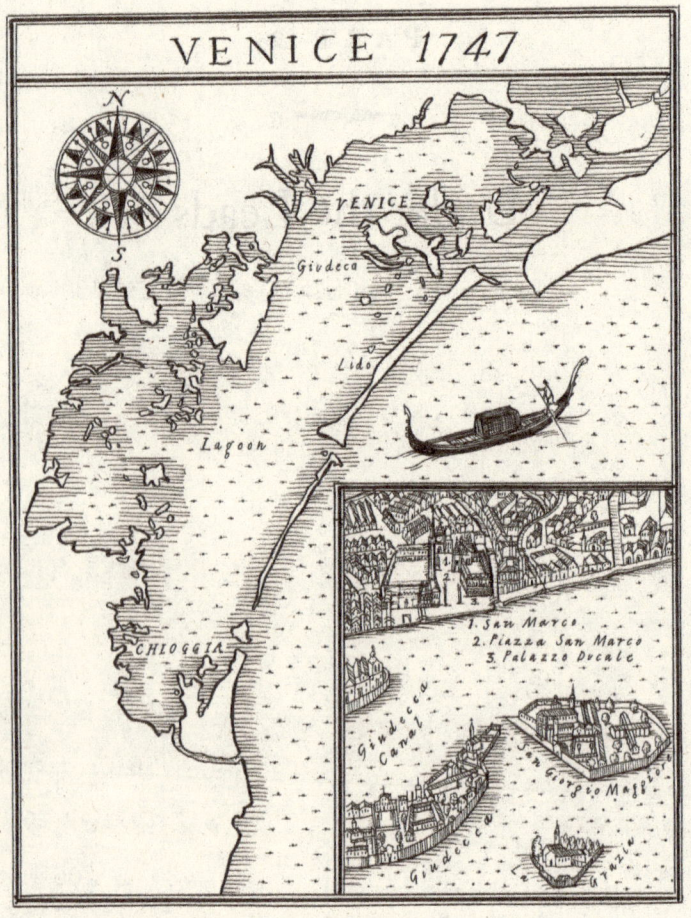

XXXV

The direct road to Rome was by sea from Marseille or, in a pinch, by Geneva and the Valdaosta. Not knowing who knew what of my mission, but fearing the worst from the nest of spies that was La Ferté-Joyeuse, I made a great bow by way of Munich and Innsbruck and came down to Venice. I believed that in the to-and-fro of Venice, I might learn something of the condition of the Stuart Court at Rome, and I had a wish to pay my respects at the tomb of my benefactor, Mr John Law of Lauriston. It was he who had first brought me to Paris where, at the Royal Bank Mr Law had founded, in the night of December 10, 1720, I first saw Jeanne de Joyeuse, as my lady was then styled, at age thirteen, returned with her father from a dancing-party at the Palace of the Tuileries. All the while, I wondered how Mme de Maurepas was faring with the foundling's syllogisms.

A habit of caution had taken me in thrall. I passed by the inn at Chioggia, and left my horse, saddle-bags and pistols at the house of a gallant lady, the famous Signorina Zulietta. Once on the chiefest island, I made my general quarter in the fine square of St Mark, at a coffee-shop named the Venice Triumphant. It was the twelfth day of May, 1747, and the holiday of Ascension was in swing.

As everybody knows, the square of St Mark is limited at its east end by the Basilica of the Evangelist and the Palace of the Duke, or Doge in Venetian. On the north and south sides are long ranges, called *procuratie*, which house divers public and ecclesiastical offices and, under shady stone arcades, shops and *caffè* such as, on the south side, the Venice Triumphant or Mr Florian's. In the middle of the western side, flanked by arcades, was the parish church of St Geminian. Having drunk a cup of coffee, and won with maddening slowness three games of chess, I made my way to the west end of the square and the parish church. A gentleman followed me, but just a single gentleman. Mr Law's monument was in the sacristy. As I stood before it, thinking of very little at all, I sensed the gentleman beside me.

"Were you acquainted, sir, with the late Mr Law?"

That seemed more than a little curious. I kept to the matter before us. "The latinity, sir, is beyond praise."

The gentleman sighed. "Twenty-five years ago, there were shreds of learning in this place. An inebriated student from Padua scrawled for me the epitaph on a napkin at Mr Florian's. All gone, now. The history of Venice is ended. We loll in our parti-coloured ruin, startled by coffee, diverted by sermons and playing-cards, lulled by water and subsidiary arias. Were it not for the gallant ladies, who alone can separate the nobility from their sequins, there would be no commerce or industry."

I turned to see a man, plainly dressed and wigged, with a douce and candid face. He said: "I am Blondeau, merchant of the French nation at Venice."

"Hamilton, Scotch tourist. Honour'd to know ye, sir. I am here principally for my education, but I have commissions from the French ladies. Fans in the Turkish taste. Brocade. That sort of thing. Mme la marquise de Maurepas requires lenses ground to the very finest exactitudes."

"A most accomplished lady, I have heard. I believe she is quite recovered from her indisposition." He calculated a moment. "The glass-men are at Murano and we must wait on the tide. Shall we start with the *ventagli*, which are nearer at hand?"

Our progress was not rapid. M. Blondeau was known. Boys danced about him, dipping sugared almonds from his surcoat pockets. At San Moisè Profeta, a fishwife ran at him, babbling in Venetian through her tears, while he spoke to her gentle phrases. The other lady was summoned, and stood with her hands on her hips. After a while, M. Blondeau established peace and the ladies shook hands. He was consul of France, as his father in the great King's reign, and (as he hoped) his son in the next.

The fan-makers were huddled together, as in a bazar of Persia, near the church of Saint Stephen. Out of my depth, I left the choice to M. Blondeau, who, I am sure, rewarded his favourite artists. No prices were named and no money paid. Once out in the square, M. Blondeau told me of my benefactor and how, broken by his wanderings and fearful for his life, he had come in the winter of 'Twenty-seven to Venice. He had with him only his son, a lad of about twenty. They lived on cow's milk. The foreigners of condition shunned Mr Law, but the Messrs Inquisitors placed confidential men about him, while the English resident and the French ambassador dogged him across every bridge and down every vennel. Everybody believed that, before the Royal Bank at Paris had stopped that December night of 1720, he had spirited a fortune out of France. In reality, M. Blondeau said, he had but a diamond of poor water which he used to place on the table to meet a wager.

"He came to me because he did not trust His Excellency the Ambassador of France with his letters. We became friends. He had an idea to buy some pictures to send to Holland so that his wife and son and daughter might have an inheritance. For an Englishman, his eye was not bad, and Signor Zanetti and Signorina Rosalba had pity on him, and gave him advice. It was I who emballed the pictures and arranged the marine insurance."

He took me under an arch into a shady courtyard.

"This is the Palazzo Dandolo. About a hundred years ago, the Council of Ten became concerned that the nobility was ruining itself in play in taverns and under arcades. Wishing to control a passion that it could not suppress, it gave Signor Dandolo the right to convene a public gaming-house, but under the condition that only noble men might hold the bank at basset and faro. At first, M. Law formed little companies with *barnabotti*, that is, the decayed noble gentlemen who live in San Barnaba. When the English started coming for the music in the

Carneval season, M. Law took a table at Florian's in the morning, and would offer the young men every sort of hazard."

"Did you note any of them, M. Blondeau?"

"Yes, but I am no arithmetician. I remember M. Law offered Milord Ponsonby ten thousand sequins if he could throw six sixes with the dies, but if the lord was unsuccessful, he must pay a sequin."

"If that is a true recollection, M. Blondeau, Mr Law would, in time, have had a cart of Raffaels. The odds appear very much to favour him. By about five times."

"I think the English young gentlemen were happy to lose a few sequins so that they could go home and say that they had played at Venice with the famous M. Law. Then, before Advent in the year 'Twenty-eight, M. Law asked me to find some rooms for him for his own place or, as we call it, *ridotto*. There, the three windows up the first pair of stairs."

By some itinerary, not detected by me but by the design to M. Blondeau, we had doubled back to the square of St Mark, and were facing Saint Geminian. I followed M. Blondeau's outstretched arm to a set of windows, indistinguishable from their companions.

"May we go up?"

"Alas! The rooms have been placed under seal. They were small but convenient. Behind the two windows to your left was the games room, and then the window on your right was the ladies' drawing-room, where they might mask or make repairs to their toilette. At the back was a *bottega di caffè*. The games were faro and roulette. Mr Law held the faro bank."

"Did you have a share, M. Blondeau?"

He did not hear my question, but continued his memorial. "With the new year, M. Law began to win and win and win. By day, young William Law and I, and Signor Zanetti the Younger, bargained for pictures at the Grassi sale and paid in warm cash. Then, at the height of Carneval, we had snow and such a gale of wind that nobody dared go out, the gondolas foundered in the Canal, and a lady of quality and her maid had to be rescued with hooks. M. Law fell ill with a cold, which spread to his chest. The news was in the coffee-shops in half-an-hour. M. Gergy, the Ambassador of France, and Colonel Burges, the English Resident, sent men to camp on the stairs, and came in person so that, in the end, I was obliged to say that the patient was too weak to receive them.

"M. Law was in good spirits. He said that his death now could not but be of service to his family. On Ash

Wednesday, in the evening, M. Gergy returned with a Jesuit, Father Origi, to hear M. Law's confession. Young M. William stayed in the chamber but though the good father pressed him hard, M. Law revealed nothing. After the confessor had left, M. Law called me to his pillow and bade me hold the pictures in secret until I could sell them for his family's advantage. He died in the Roman Catholic faith."

"Why did not the Ambassador or Mr Burges impound the pictures for the King of France and Mr Law's other creditors?"

The Consul did not hear my question.

I said: "M. Blondeau, will you be so kind as to recommend to me a confessor? I wish to abjure the Protestant sect."

"Most admirable!"

After a while, he said: "I have heard that Mme la marquise de Maurepas plays the French spinet to perfection."

I said nothing.

"The best man is Father Bianchi, the parish priest at St Geminian. He is by no means inquisitive. We shall call on him after the Festival."

"I was thinking of this after-dinner."

"I fear you must continue damned for a little longer."

We were like two men-of-war, beating against the wind, always a cannon-shot apart, each captain reluctant to show colour.

"And then shall we dine?"

"Will you not see the portrait of me done in crayons by the divine Rosalba?"

"Of course, M. Blondeau."

"Truly, she is a great painter, and a great heart and soul. In matters pertaining to her art, there is nothing she cannot do."

I woke from my watery slumber. I saw that, out of my habitual parsimony, I had confined myself to fans and catechisms, while M. Blondeau sought a more valuable commerce with my patroness. He wished my lady to buy Mr Law's pictures. Any man of the world would long ago have caught the drift. I pulled myself together. I said: "Mme la marquise de Maurepas has for some time been dissatisfied with the altar-piece in the principal chapel of La Ferté-Joyeuse. The late duke her father decorated the shrine in a spirit more of magnificence than of devotion. As to the side-altars, least said, soonest mended."

M. Blondeau nodded and then, without alteration of tone or manner, said: "There is word that a Scottish officer is travelling to Rome with something of great price for the Pretender. Sufficient to raise an army and arm a fleet. It is possible that you met that man at an inn or toll-bar. Tyrell here, Smith at Turin, Cockerill at Genoa have instructions to do the man an ill turn on the road, and at all costs stop him reaching the Papal Territories, where the English have no resident."

He went on in his crinkum-crankum way. "At Rome, the principal man of music is Galuppi. He performs at the opera and at the palace of the King of England. I sent his last toccata to madame." He began to beat out the tune, which I recognised. "Galuppi always needs singers and players. Now, let us dine, M. Hamilton. Do you eat stewed crabs with laurel leaves?"

"Only on high occasions, M. Blondeau."

As we made our way to the head of the square, I glanced up to see a cable stretched at half a right-angle from the loggia of the bell-tower to His Most Excellency the Doge's balcony on the principal floor of the Palace. To say something, and to defer for a moment the mess of crabs, I asked:

"What is that great rope, M. Blondeau?"

"It is a Venetian tradition, the which, like all our traditions, is of recent establishment. Last year, two men with wooden swords fought upon the cable. We can still put on a spectacle, better than any city on earth. With all eyes on the sky, it is a high day for the ancient and respectable guild of cut-purses."

XXXVI

The practice of masking the face, which the Venetians must have witnessed in the East and then turned to a contrary purpose, was permitted for all fifteen days of the festival and served as a veil for the libertinage that was the substitute for freedom in the Most Serene Republic. Under the mask, each woman became Helen of Troy and each man Achilles or, at the least, Paris. It was stated, in some ordinance that became ancient the moment it was inked, that masks were not to be worn until after Vespers, but that was ignored.

Among the foreigners thronging the square was a peloton of young Englishmen. They had brought with them their dogs and fowling-pieces, but were, I jaloused, in the hunt for sweeter sport. One asked me at Mr Florian's, in a whisper, if it were true that the ladies of Venice were far from cruel.

I was sure they had been warned by their tutors to shun Scottish men of my age of life, blasted by sun, stone-poor, well-armed, knocked-about and at ease in the languages and customs of the country. Yet they sought me out. I asked myself if they even knew they were Mr Tyrell's secret agents. That gentleman's scheme, I believe, was that, in pursuit of one or t'other sport, we should repair to one of the distant islands in the marsh, where I might be made to disappear. I could not guide the lads in the field, as it were, but I took them to *Tigrane* at the Theatre of Sant'Angelo, where they stood like farm-hands in the pit and whistled the singers, without partiality.

As was my settled routine, the next morning at ten I was taking my coffee at Mr Florian's. I looked up from the *avvisi*, which are a sort of gazettes. A courier in the livery of the French Ambassador stood with his hand on his hip, proffering a letter.

There was no salutation or signature.

The letter read:

> *Intelligence reaches her from Rome that there is a design of evil against the lives of King James of England and the Prince of Wales. There are letters out to arrest a certain Col. Nelson, a desperado who lost his men and*

his reason in the fight at Invernesse. His Holiness has set a guard of twenty-four Swiss at the palace of the King of England, Piazza dei Santi Apostoli. She asks M. Hamilton to have a care of that man. For reasons of which M. Hamilton is unaware, she cannot journey to Italy to share his pleasures and diversions, as is her deepest wish. She sends a bill for 1,000 sequins, money of Venice, on M. Blondeau, consul of France at that Court, payable at sight and all charges comprised, and requests that M. Hamilton expedite his business in Italy and return among his friends, where he may dig canals and smoke pipes where he pleases, and never be separated from those friends till God decrees it.

PS: A gentleman of Dunkerque has submitted factures comprising 250,000 livres for carriage from the isles, 720 livres and 6 sols for lead and powder, and 9 livres 8 sols for surgery. She has paid those charges. May she ask M. Hamilton that, in the pleasant land of Italy, he practise a more severe economy?

Every blade and sharper in the den was watching me. Good Blondeau was in the doorway. As I passed him, he said: "Tyrell is this moment come from the College."

"Would you kindly settle my account with Mr Florian? Against the security of the *ventagli*?"

Out in the square, I drew sword. The tumblers and mountebanks scattered like pigeons at a shot. As I walked towards the Duke's Palace, through drifts of streamers and sugared almonds, I turned over in my mind my lady's letter. Not for the first time, I marvelled at the efficiency of the English. With just a little false information, they had enlisted not just the Jacks, but also His Holiness, in the project of killing me and capturing or abolishing the jewel.

There was in my lady's letter some elation, some well of happiness that bubbled up amid the peril and expense. What were those reasons of which I was unaware? And if that deep-died pirate Douvry charges His Very Christian Majesty 100,000 francs to carry a ton of gun-powder through the English line-of-battle, why must my lady pay him two-and-one-half times that to pick up a litter-patient from a desert beach of Barra while H.M. Frigates *Thetis* and *Arethusa* pop away to no great effect? All the more, as Mme de Maurepas keeps to her pecuniary engagements and the King of France does not.

Before the palace, a detachment of the constables called *sbirri* was forming in raggedy order. From the arcades of the *procuratie* on the basine side, there was a jingling of boots and muskets. Ahead of me, the young officer had his men in line. He inclined his head, as if to say: We are not much, Colonel, but sufficient, with the enfilading fire from the side, to make a cullender of you.

I reversed my sword, which he accepted with a compliment, which I returned. On the steps, a nobleman in robes and full-bottomed wig was reading aloud some Latin drivel. Against the wall, a gentleman, dressed as a squire of the English Midlands out with his pack, lounged at ease, his surcoat open on his pistols. I presumed that was Mr Tyrell. He looked a rough subject. Two bravos, stinking of excrement and raw shallots, bound my hands and blindfolded me. I thought: Why is my mistress so happy? We passed up stairs, cold, wet and narrow, that sometimes went one way, sometimes another. I stumbled against a wall which lowered my blind-fold a peep. At the topmost landing-place, we passed into a large and dirty garret, where a skylight revealed bundles of old papers and presses. In front was a transe or corridore lit by two grilled windows, facing to the east, for I marked the church of San Zaccaria and, in the distance, the basine and fabricks of the Arsenale.

Once in India, an experimented man told me that with

each minute of captivity the prospect of escape diminishes. As we passed down the corridore, I tripped and, as one of the men steadied me, I sprang up and dashed my head into the base of his chin. There was quite a braul but even Hercules, the ancients used to say, cannot fight against two, and I am not Hercules. I curled up, seeking only to protect a part of my lower person that I had come of late somewhat to value. After a time, the bravos became puff'd and dragg'd me into a cell and bolted the door on me.

In no condition to stand or move, I exercised my arithmetical reason. For good M. Blondeau to send an express to my lady: six days. For Mme de Maurepas to take coach to the palace of Versailles: two days. For my lady to storm at His Majesty in full company: half-an-hour. For the Minister of Foreign Affairs to draft, sign and despatch a courier to M. le comte de Montaigu, ambassador of France at the Court of the Most Serene Republic: ten days. For Mr Montaigu to stamp up to the College in high resentment: half an hour. For the College to request from Their Excellencies the Council of Ten the favour of my release: one day. For the Council of Ten to consider the request and then instruct the Three Chiefs: one day. That meant that I would be free in a little under three weeks, or, rather, that I would be dead before then. Because of my reputation for truculence, it is likely Mr Tyrell would engage two assassins. It would mean also, because of the press of time, that the men might not be the flower or creame of their ancient profession.

My chamber was a sort of hutch, made of oaken panels reinforced with iron. I am five feet and ten inches in length, and I could not stand upright. Certain impressions from the Castle of the Bastille, which I had thought long erased, arose in my mind, but I fought them off. I was not a friendless boy but an officer of the King of France in good standing. My tutelary goddess would not forsake me.

I slept on the floor in half-hour relays, for the bells of St Mark might have been in my cell. I woke for the last time at the third hour, Venetian time, bathed in a ravishing light, sparkling off the basine of St Mark and the white stone of Istria. A delicious breeze came in through the two windows on the far side of the transe. I thought: This could have been very much worse.

XXXVII

I had expected the concierge of the prisons of the Council of Ten at Venice to be a man of distinction. Signor Lodovico was not such a man.

"You are fortunate, English sir, that the console of France has given me a very little money for your entertainment. My wife was at first light at the fish market in the Rialto and is, at this very moment, dressing for you the very best squid gonads."

"Dear Signor Lodovico, my delicate state of health places an embargo on such delicacies. A dish of maccheroni, with a very little butter, if cheap, and a sprinkle of the cheese of Parma; fruit and green stuff of the season; and a splash of Cyprus wine to moisten it all *et sufficit*."

"Not the octopus lungs?"

"Alas! Let us cast up our account at the end of each month, where any costs saved in my forgaeing your palustrine dainties might contribute towards Masses for the soul of good M. Blondeau, and a present to your lady."

Like many men who are devious and ignorant, Signor Lodovico thought I was the same: indeed, that the whole world, from Their Most Excellencies downward, was constituted of such men. He could not believe that I was so simple, or that I trusted him to have the Masses said. Then, perhaps, he remembered I was a foreigner and that foreigners were strange.

"In return, dear friend, will you request Their Excellencies permit me to walk for half an hour each day in the garret, so that I can stand up straight and rest my wounds?"

"Impossible."

"Signor Lodovico! I know you wish only to be of use to the Serene Republic and serve the glorious evangelist Saint Mark. From all that you have told me, I believe that I shall be of better service to the both alive, rather than dead."

"The French console will provide necessities."

"In which case, I would prefer to have a bed with its linen, a chair, seven Holland shirts, a comb, mirror, razor—"

"Not permitted."

". . . ink-glass, paper, pen—"

"Forbidden."

". . . and a large Latin Bible, with majuscule print, for the light is not good in here."

XXXVIII

From Signor Lodovico, I learned something of the criminal police of the Most Serene Republic. In the early years, malefactors had been confined in cells beneath the west wing of the palace, which cells had become known, inaccurately as Signor Lodovico contended, as the Pozzi or Wells. It is true that the apartments could be moist, especially at high tide, where a grille of one foot square placed to attract fresh air at times admitted sea-water and rats, but the prisoner's bed was raised some two feet from the floor and there was a shelf yet higher for his or her possessions.

About one hundred and fifty years ago, in the more enlightened sixteenth century of our salvation, the Council of Ten had decreed that the conditions of confinement should be made less rigorous, and more light and air, less sea-water, and fewer rats admitted to the cells so as to preserve the prisoners in health and promote by kindness, in so far as that was possible, an awakening of their sense of duty. New cells had been erected in a corner of the Chancellery, which, because they sat directly beneath the leads of the roof, had become known as the Leads or, in Venetian, I Piombi. Since then, the wisdom of their Most Excellencies had advanced yet further and they had set on foot a modern prison, called the New Prisons or Le Quattro, across the rio or little canal to the east and connecting to the chamber of the Council of Ten by a bridge of white Istria. Signor Lodovico said that the bridge, for no reason he could think on, had become nick-named the Ponte dei Sospiri or Bridge of Sighs.

"However, that house is not for a foreign gentleman such as yourself, but for common criminals, thieves and suchlike."

"Am I not a common criminal, Signor Lodovico?"

"Oh no."

"So what is my offence? It must indeed have been grave, for me to be so confined half-way to heaven."

"It is not necessary for you to know. Their Most Excellencies know, and that is all that is required."

"So that is all well, then." I paused. "Do many men make their escape from this prison?"

Signor Lodovico made a false laugh. "And how would they do so?"

"Perhaps, through the floor."

"Beneath us the Saloon of the Messrs Inquisitors."

"Then through the ceiling."

"The palace is roofed with plates of lead three foot square and more than an inch in thickness."

"A strong man might push one of the plates aside."

"Then what, my brave English sir? The slope of the roof is three feet down for one across. A man cannot stand on it."

"I have seen, in my saunters about town, chimneys and seven or eight sky-lights. A determined man might break through those."

"They are barred with grilles of iron."

"He might jump down into the canal on this side and swim to safety."

"It is a fall of ninety feet, and the water of the rio is but three feet in depth, which is not sufficient to cushion a fall from so great a height. The villain would break legs or back or neck."

"What about the side of the courtyard?"

"It is incessantly patrolled by guards from the Arsenale."

"And further, facing the Piazza?"

"It being the feast of Sensa, it is full at all hours with revellers. If they saw a man upon the roof, they would instantly alert the constables."

"So, Signor Lodovico, only a very few have successfully made their escape?"

"None, Mr English, in two hundred and fifty years."

Since my principal concern was not to get out, but to ensure that nobody got in, I found Signor Lodovico's brag and boast reassuring. He said: "Do men escape in England?"

"Oh yes. There the prisons are just bad inns, managed for profit. By some arrangement of business, or the exchange of mercenary offices, a prisoner's friends may easily achieve his enlargement."

"That is impossible here."

Signor Lodovico seemed rather to regret the rigours of the Venetian system, and hanker after the commercial to-and-fro of Great Britain. Had he but the chance, he would sell Saint Mark for a groat. I lost some of my good temper.

The concierge himself received the key to the cells from the secretary of the Messrs Inquisitors at dawn, and must return it within one hour. One thus dined at the beginning of the day, reserving some portion of the feast for the evening.

XXXIX

While his men jointed my bed, I learned from Signor Lodovico that after the Ascension Day, which we call at Venice the Sensa, there was always a vacation of three days, in which their Most Excellencies made their villegiature on the firm ground. I saw that I had less time than I had hoped. What I needed above all was a weapon.

I had bespoke a lectern Bible not simply for my edification but so that M. Blondeau might conceal in its binding a sharp tool such as a surgeon's trocart or what men call in Italy a *stiletto*. On reflection, I saw I was demanding too much of that good man who would be lothe to risk for an untried friend and the commerce of Mme de Maurepas a position in the Republic that his father had earned and that he hoped to pass to his son. As it turned out, the Holy Book contained no such profane enclosure and I wished I had asked in its place for the love-letters of Signorina Franco.

"Good news! Their Most Clement Excellencies have consented to allow you to walk at dawn for half an hour outside your cell. I shall attend you."

Of this privilege I made much use. The place where the cells were erected had once been some adjunct of the Chancellery, and bore traces of its pristine employment in a range of wormey cupboards and document presses. From the light that came through the bars of the skylight above, I was able to study these papers and learned, in the masses of mouse-eaten screed, something of the government of the Duchy of Candia in the thirteenth century. That island, the ancient Krete or Creta, appeared to be a most happy place.

The doors of the cabinets were hung on iron hinges, but the wood had decayed in the salt air and the nails that held the schank of one hinge were loose. It happened that Signor Lodovico was called away, and I ripped off the schank and placed it in my breeks. For the first time, my limping gait came into service. In taking my dinner that day, by a mishap I broke the bowl that held my maccheroni. In the long hours till dawn the next day, I used the sherds to make a point and blade on the shaft. By inserting rags into that nail-cavity nearest the base of the schank, I fashioned a rude poignet or hand and the whole contraption resembled somewhat a legionnarie's short sword or *ensis* of ancient Rome. With this makeshift arm beside me in my cot, I slept as sweetly as by my mistress.

How I dreamed under the Leads of Venice! I seemed to fly above the earth, or limped through teeming cities that jostled and amalgamated, so that in the press of foot-passengers or the turning of a street-corner, Edinburgh became Calcutta. I tumbled in a harness of bells and water-light. One night, some fifteen days after my confinement, I dreamed of a vast, unclouded sky. Beneath me was a river, wider than any I had seen in Europe and India. Woods of pine and fir covered the banks and extended as far as the eye could reach. On the horizon, at the limit of sight, were the stone walls of a city. Before me were my Irish men, but not as they were on the moor, but red from the wind and sun, or dark as mahogany, and every one of them piqued and daubed with paint or fluttering with feathers. Never had I felt such a sensation of liberty and of happiness.

I cried out: "Yes, there, but not yet! Give me a year with Jeannette and the orphan!"

"What are you saying, Mr English?"

Somebody was speaking through the wall.

I said: "I was dreaming. That is all."

"Well, are ye coming, or do we leave ye?"

We.

"I am not armed."

"We are."

Armed.

I said to myself: That dream came through the Gate of Horn and I shall outlive this fight. I took up the schank and, to mask it, threw my cloak over my right arm.

I heard the lock groan. In the lantern-light, I saw three men. The affair was becoming serious. I needed to save my life. The first man came on, saw my covered right arm, raised his head and cracked it on the ceiling-beam. I plunged my sword into his throat. He fell back and, as he did so, the next chap saw my reeking weapon. From the spitting blood, the cell was as hot as a furnace.

When there is a great preponderance of force, there is nothing more certain to sap the courage than its immediate reduction by half. The man before me had but a stiletto. I said:

"Drop your knife and I shall spare you."

It was no good. The man behind him was pushing him forward. He had no choice but to strike, but he was encumbered by his dying compagnon. I stabbed him in the arm-pit and he fell, breaking my old blade in two. The third man stood aghast in the doorway.

"Drop your knife and I shall spare you."

He did so. That was fortunate, for myself I had no edged weapon.

"Attend to your brother."

"How?"

"Oh, for the love of God."

My make-shift blade had passed through the second man's shoulder. I bandaged it as best as I might, gathered the fallen knives, and picked up my hat.

"What is your name, sir?"

"No name."

"Weel, Signor No-Name, you and I shall now leave this place."

Outside the cell, I saw a hempen rope thick as ship cord and, following it upwards, felt a gust of air and saw starlight. One of the plates of lead had been moved aside. I could not descry Mr Tyrell's plan, so I must, like a fractious child, seek every opposite.

"You go first."

No-Name shook his head.

"Get up! Or I shall deal with you as I dealt with your friends."

Once in the open air, I saw the rope in my hands was tied to the grille of a lucarne or sky-light, while a second rope from the same attachment hung down over the roof on the east side. It appeared that that the ropes had been tied from inside the Palace, with or without the knowledge of the Messrs Inquisitors. I pushed and prodded my friend, hand over hand, to the sky-light, whose back-side made a tolerable resting-place. After a while, I said: "Now, descend."

"You are to go first."

"Am I?"

I gave him a thorough kick. Just in time, he found the rope and then was dropping in giant steps. He vanished beyond the parapet. Then, the rope in my hands went limp and, at the same instant, I heard a pistol-shot. I pulled up the rope and stowed it ship-shape behind the sky-light. Poor fellow, I thought, but that ball was destined for me. Mr Tyrell does not care for the diamond, just so long as it is not with me or with King James. Perhaps, he would have retrieved it from my body in the rio and made himself a Versailles at Bushey or Saint Albans. Or left the thing to lie with Gaspara Stampa in the Venetian mud.

XL

I took stock. The place of greatest safety was amid the domes of the Basilica, where there was sure to be a door or grating I could force. I did not like the look of it. The shrine was illuminated for the Festival, and though I thought myself safe from a pistol shot, I was a dead man from the long gun. I resolved to take the opposite course, into the darkness towards the basine. The long rope was too heavy for me to bear. I untied the smaller rope, coiled it from shoulder to hip, and set off along the roof-ridge to the south.

As I chevauched along the ridge, I had a recollection that seemed to arise not in my mental faculties but in my lower portions. There I was again, in Paris in the year 'Twenty, under the chestnut trees, inching in winter sunshine along the wall of the Royal Bank. That was the day I first saw Jeanne de Joyeuse at her age thirteen and I became, for better or for worse, a Frenchman and a lover of women.

I reached the end of the range and turned to the west. Out in the basine, the stern-lights of boats bobbed and hotched on the tide. As I wraggled towards the music and laughter in the square, I cursed the founders of the Serene Republic for their magnificence. Was it necessary that the Hall of the Greater Council beneath me should be so infernally long? The whole history of this famous city was playing out in my arse. In the square before me, they must have lit a feu-de-joie or bonfire. In the red light dancing off the bell-tower, I saw the cable on which M. Blondeau's acrobates had fought. I thought: Why is Providence so good to me?

And not better. Here there was no sky-light, not even one chimney-stack, to which to tie my good rope. All that

I could see in the flickering lights was the lip of the roof, formed of crenells or battlements in the Saracen style. I made to descend on my back but at once lost my hold and slid. I pushed out my heels to catch the crenells, but they crumbled like paper, and in a roaring and a swirl of light and falling brick, I was tumbling into the piazza of St Mark.

Something struck me in the chest and face. I thought it was an angel, sent to arrest my fall, but I was rising in a spin, as in the ship-wreck of the *Prince-de-Conty*, though in air not water. I was falling again, and saw the cable and spread myself like a cat. This time, the blow was to my stomach. I rose again. My legs were of no use, but my upper parts still had some strength, and I caught the cord under my right arm-pit. Then with a rolling of every muscle from chin to toe, I pulled the rest of me astride. From below, there was a patter of applause and, here and there, cries of *Bravo!*

That Providence which had preserved me had preserved also my hat. Taking it off with my right hand, I raised it to Saint Mark; with my left, to the sea on that side; and with both hands to my public at the front. There was renewed applause, and then the crowd began to thin in quest of newer amusement.

With difficulty, I turned about so I was pointing downhill. Below me, at a distance of some ten or fifteen yards, was a balcony with statues on each side, embodying Mars and Neptune, of the very finest Gothick art. I wriggled down, swung over the baluster, pulled open a door set with panes of glass, and came into the largest room I had ever seen. Clerks were working at tables by candle-light. A group of men in red robes were pacing the tiled floor.

I said in French: "Bernsdorff. Dane tourist. Dead lost. Would you be so civil as to point me to the Basilica of St Mark?"

A gentleman raised his arm to a door in front of me, and I strode out and down a turnpike stair. At the landing place, I heaved a sigh, as if I had escaped a great danger, which I indeed had. My legs were in a horrid wobble. I came out in an arcade or loggia, open to the court, which I remembered to be the first or noble floor of the palace. On the far side, towards the basilica, two lamps revealed a staircase with giant statues at its four corners which I took to be the ceremonial entrance to the Doge's apartments. I flitted between the columns like a lame ghost. At the base of the great staircase, I pushed at a door which groaned open. I smelled wax and incense and, to my surprise, fine ladies. I had reached the famous basilica of St Mark.

I could see in the flickering lights was the lip of the roof, formed of crenells or battlements in the Saracen style. I made to descend on my back but at once lost my hold and slid. I pushed out my heels to catch the crenells, but they crumbled like paper, and in a roaring and a swirl of light and falling brick, I was tumbling into the piazza of St Mark.

Something struck me in the chest and face. I thought it was an angel, sent to arrest my fall, but I was rising in a spin, as in the ship-wreck of the *Prince-de-Conty*, though in air not water. I was falling again, and saw the cable and spread myself like a cat. This time, the blow was to my stomach. I rose again. My legs were of no use, but my upper parts still had some strength, and I caught the cord under my right arm-pit. Then with a rolling of every muscle from chin to toe, I pulled the rest of me astride. From below, there was a patter of applause and, here and there, cries of *Bravo!*

That Providence which had preserved me had preserved also my hat. Taking it off with my right hand, I raised it to Saint Mark; with my left, to the sea on that side; and with both hands to my public at the front. There was renewed applause, and then the crowd began to thin in quest of newer amusement.

With difficulty, I turned about so I was pointing downhill. Below me, at a distance of some ten or fifteen yards, was a balcony with statues on each side, embodying Mars and Neptune, of the very finest Gothick art. I wriggled down, swung over the baluster, pulled open a door set with panes of glass, and came into the largest room I had ever seen. Clerks were working at tables by candle-light. A group of men in red robes were pacing the tiled floor.

I said in French: "Bernsdorff. Dane tourist. Dead lost. Would you be so civil as to point me to the Basilica of St Mark?"

A gentleman raised his arm to a door in front of me, and I strode out and down a turnpike stair. At the landing place, I heaved a sigh, as if I had escaped a great danger, which I indeed had. My legs were in a horrid wobble. I came out in an arcade or loggia, open to the court, which I remembered to be the first or noble floor of the palace. On the far side, towards the basilica, two lamps revealed a staircase with giant statues at its four corners which I took to be the ceremonial entrance to the Doge's apartments. I flitted between the columns like a lame ghost. At the base of the great staircase, I pushed at a door which groaned open. I smelled wax and incense and, to my surprise, fine ladies. I had reached the famous basilica of St Mark.

In contradistinction to the system of Persia, where assassins and fornicators may live out their days unscaithed, honoured and stuffed with alms in the mosque of Isfahan, there is no sanctuary at Venice, whether against criminal or civil pursuit, even in so sacral a temple as the Basilica of St Mark. There was no refuge for me except outside the confines of the Serene Republic. Instead, I wished to rest my legs, and allow my chafed hands and arse, which I had hitherto mummed and silenced, to make their complaints and have their say. I wished also to thank God.

I knelt and prayed: "Lord, of all the scrapes in my life, that was the worst and yet you have saved me. I do not know why you preserve me when you have taken better men, but if you could extend your grace to bring me to the south and to the terra firma, I will attempt to mend my ways, swear less and pray more. Anyway, let Your will be done."

Then a second miracle occurred. The young lady beside me, disgusted by my prison stink and the blood on my face and shirt, or (alas!) simply by my person, moved away to join a party at another box. No man, however advanced in years, blackened by sun, battered by shot, and holed in his breeks, likes to see a young lady's back. I glanced in shame at her empty place to see that she had left behind a numbered token of brass.

At the guard-robe by the western door, I received a cloak, a tri-corn hat and the mask called a moretta. I said to the servant:

"Please tell my daughter that I await her on the steps. She has my purse."

The sweet scent of the cloak, and the bead in my mouth that held the mask in place, caused me to swoon. As I glided through the crowd in the direction of the Mole, I took care to make only the smallest steps and to keep my hands concealed. I fancy I attracted not a few appreciating glances. If, as the Hindous say, we have some other lives, I would like at some period of my transmigration to be a pretty woman and smell like a hedgerow in April and catch the eye of all.

At the Mole, a boatman sprang up and stood to his oar.

"And where do you go, my pretty masque?"

I raised my head in the direction of the terra firma, gathered up my cloak, brushed off his hand, and stepped down as winsomely as I might on the cushions under the canopy.

"Chioggia! But that is five leagues against the tide!"

I stood up and made to step out.

"Come now, my beauty. Sit. Sit. You will find, as other ladies have discovered, that Bertuccio Caravello, alone of the brotherhood of boatmen of Venice, can ply his oar all night."

With relief, I saw the jetty recede and with it the sound of laughter and music. The plash of the oar soothed me into feminine languor. Signor Bertuccio had settled into a circular sweep, even and slow, so as to conserve his strength. We passed the dark shape of St George the Greater and felt the wind off the lagune.

"Will you not speak, my Ninetta?"

He burst into song.

"*Belle parole*
Co' le xe sole . . ."

I confess I could not resist joining in, pitching my voice into the contr'alto register. From there we progressed to "Cara Nina" and "Che granxi", the songs becoming each time more licentious, so that when Bertuccio launched into "Un anguilleta fresca", I turned my back on him. Now was no time nor place for Signor Bertuccio's fresh eel. We sulked as we swept along beside the sand-bed called the Lido, while on our tribord side a lamp or cooking fire lit up rickle-rackle fishermen's huts on stilts. When I saw the sailors' lantern on the bell-tower of the high church of Chioggia, I piped up with "No te par ora" and we were friends again. The tide had turned and the boat skimmed the sea as if it had been a mill-race. We approached the piazza of Chioggia. Mr Bertuccio bowed and drew in oar to pass under the bridge, but I gestured for him to proceed up the side canal where the Dominicans are building their convent.

When he saw Signorina Zulietta's jetty, Mr Bertuccio all but burst from his skin. I alighted with delicacy, did a half-turn, put my cloaked hand to my lips, and tripped up the garden without a backward glance. Once in door, I threw off my duds, and took the stair in fours.

"Signorina Zulietta! Give me a girl! I must have a girl!"

That lady was stretched on a divano, in her linen, smoking a pipe. She rose in somersault and fell back again.

"Sweet Mary and Jesus! Have you been eating cuttle-fish? You had better have Barbarina."

"No, you wretch. The lass is for my gondolere. Where is my pocket-book?"

She reached under her bottom for my purse. I took out a hot sequin.

"Here is Miss Barbarina's fee. The man is dying for her at the jetty. And for you, Signorina Zulietta, for the care of my horse and purse, for your fair face, and your unbreakable discretion, are five gold pistoles."

"I would rather a kiss."

"A kiss is only a kiss, Mlle Zulietta. Money will buy you anything that can be bought, including a kiss."

My gold vanished into the same cosie treasure or banco.

My horse was starving and my purse light, and I doubted whether Zulietta's discretion were not overdrawn. The jewel was where I had concealed it. I thought it prudent that, rather than take the short road to the Pope's territories by Ferrare and Ravenna, I should make a deviation through Vicenza, Modena and Florence, throwing the cloak here, the hat there and the mask in a third place, so they might never be re-united. So ended my life as a woman.

XLI

I jacked and dawdled on the road. In Florence, I assisted at the Grand Duke's levy and gawped at holy pictures. Once my mount was rested, I rode up the River Arno so as to come to Bologna from the south. The weather was fine and thorn-trees were white amid the small fields. After the castle of Poppi, the road passed into beech-woods. My horse could scarcely find its way between the crags and the stream. The old soldier in me thought it a capital place to lie in ambush.

My illusions fell away. I dismounted and put my ear to the ground. I could hear nothing above the rumble of the water. Then I heard the jingle of harness.

I turned off the road, and climbed through the beech-trees. Ahead of me, an arm of the hill had caused the river to mend its course. Dismounting, I climbed to the head of the ridge and looked down on what appeared at some time to have been a quarry and, ambushed there, armed and alert, six mounted men. Behind me, I could hear the tap and jingle of the approaching troop. I was pinned, as it were, between the hammer and the anvil. Really, I could not fault Mr Tyrell for industry in King George's service.

I was in a quandary. Above me, the woods thinned and I would have no cover on the bare rock. I might try to circle behind the men who had trailed me, but I doubted that I would be seen and dropped by a musket-ball.

Then I remembered M. Dalouhe's viatickes. I delved into my saddle bags and pulled out two round entities in bags of waxed cloth. On inspection, I saw they were bombshells or grenados, fashioned from ten-pound round shot from the Wars of Religion or who knows when. There must have been dozens of such boulets lying around in the magazines at La Ferté-Joyeuse. From a plug there was a hemp slowmatch dipped in what smelled like beef-tallow. I struck my tinder.

Whatever it was, it was not beef-tallow. The fuse raced and it was all I could do to cast the thing into the air. There was a flash and a blast fit to wake the hills. From out of the smoke, a hail of metal like bees from an upturned hive engulfed us. Climbing to my knees, I cast the second bomb high towards the hill where it could do no harm.

I waited for the sound of horses' feet to subside, picking rusty metal from my mount's flanks and from my hands and cheeks. As far as I could determine, Pierre Dalouhe had swept the smithy at La Ferté-Joyeuse of every nail and bolt dropped there over fifty years. I descended on foot to the quarry to attend to the wounded of the rixe, but found only one man, wand'ring in circles, with blood in his eyes, and a horse gushing blood from the throat. The man, who spoke neither French nor Italian, had a splinter of the bomb casing in the small of his back, which I cut out. I gave him brandy and a couple of florins. The poor beast I shot through the head. About the whole enterprise, there was something exotic, even oriental. It did not have the stamp of English workmanship. I wondered if they were His Holiness' men.

Not expecting further inconvenience, I set off uphill and passed into papal territory at Bologna, where Signor Cambiale, of Fratelli Cambiale, cashed Mme la marquise's bill without word. He had most of the money back, for in his back-shop he had a fiddle, by Nicholas Amati of Cremona, which would serve my purpose and a great deal more.

XLII

Once in the great city of Rome, I called on Maestro Galuppi, who was in the choir of what they call the New Church. I waited out the choral exercises, and then followed him into the sacristy. I took his toccata at Mme la marquise's break-neck speed.

At the end, Master Galuppi said: "Why do you people play so slowly?"

I offered him the instrument, but he shook his head as if, in taking it, he might not be able to return it. He said: "You might have been a player, had you applied yourself to music in place of dissipation. You may play with the seconds. The wage is one scudo per performance. Nobody minds the second violins."

As at Venice, I made my general quarter in a caffè. It was in Condotta Street by the Spanish Place, and directed by a Greek from Smyrna named Nicola. The resort was frequented by King James' servants, who could not have been a jot more attentive and courteous to the tourists, contributing opera tickets, introductions to the principal Roman families, the cares of the King's own physician and, on the Sabbath, Anglican worship. Each morning for an half-hour, His Majesty's confidential secretary, Mr Edgar, made the round of the tables.

Mr Edgar was not best suited to convivial duty, for he was a sober, careful sort of man, of Caithness, I believe, out since 'Fifteen, and almost as poor as I am. I caught him casting sinful looks upon my violin. I told him that I was a Frenchman, who had played in the house orchestra of Count Schlippenhof in Courland but had wearied of the Baltic winter and was now seeking his bread in the sunshine of Italy. I named this *avatare* Joly. It seemed Mr Edgar did not believe in Mr Joly for his eye flickered toward my fiddle-case.

Mr Edgar was fond of chess and, though he had been no further to the east than Ancona, an expert player.

Our games were what we call stale-mates. Mr Edgar took no risks, attacked no baited piece, accepted every fair exchange. In the end, I might have one marauding knight or bishop or rook, while his king was barricadoed in a corner and ringed with pawns. Signor Nicola thought he, too, was a player and, as he wisked the tables, sang out suggestions or even took it on himself to move pieces. Mr Edgar was slow to anger but I feared for our host's continued existence. I doubted that the Greek's coffee-shop would be in business long. My friend spoke little but I did learn, by a sort of inadvertence on his part, that his master attended the Roman Catholic chapel in the palace but not that of his Protestant servants in the other or eastern wing.

I had long intended to abjure the religion of my fathers, for my attachment to Presbyterian Government was not so strong as my wish to please Mme de Maurepas. Father Patrick O'Crean, my Mentor on the voyage of the *Prince-de-Conty* in 'Twenty-seven, had laid in me the foundations of the Roman faith and died as one of its most faithful martyrs. Also, the Irish men I had killed on the moor were of that belief.

I made my abjuration between the hands of Signor Righetti, first cello and a priest in minor orders, in a cabaret in Transtevere. My penance was a round of brandies, or, as we call them at Rome, *grappini*. Because we were being called back to the *conversazione*, my ghostly preceptor was kind enough to baptise and confirm me in one swoop. I proposed to take my First Communion in the chapel of the Palace of the King of England the Sunday next following, but on our presenting ourselves, Signor Righetti and I, the Pope's Switzers told us that because of a design of evil against the King, only the Court and gentle servants might attend. My preceptor wished to make a fight of it, but I took him away to Signor Nicola's.

With the hot weather, the English Court went to Albano for its villegiature. We musicians passed the summer, playing here and there, and keeping good cheer. I had the leisure to think of my young friend, but I dared not write to Mlle de Joyeuse at La Ferté. The letter would certainly be opened, both by His Holiness' postal spies, and by the English agents at the frontiers of the neighbour states. I wrote instead to the child under cover to my dearest ally: Countess Bielke, who had befriended me in Persia back in 'Forty and was now (as I learned from Dr Cameron, lately returned from Saint-Petersburgh) principal lady-in-waiting to the Tsaritsa Elizabeth Petrovna.

XLIII

On the fifteenth day of September, 1747, at the New Church, Mr Galuppi told us that we were to play at the Palace of the King of England to celebrate the Cardinal's cap lately granted the Duke of York, the younger of King James' two sons. For the festivity, that man of genius had written a serenata for eight voices. As always, we played through the piece at once. At the end of the *pròva* or rehearsing, I walked alone to Transtevere and bought of a stinky apothecary's two ounces of Venetian cerussa, a species of white pigment. At a toy-smith's in Saint Laurence, I haggled a bussola or pocket-compass.

The Palace of the King, or Palazzo del Re, which had been engaged by His Holiness for King James Stuart and his Court, stood on the Piazza of the Holy Apostles. The garden where we were to play, for we were in whole strength with percussions, lay on the north side, separated from the palace proper by a narrow lane spanned by a covered bridge. From the bridge, a turnpike stair led down into the garden so that the Royal Family and its servants need not expose themselves to vulgar eyes in the alley.

The place was illuminated like the Fair and a fountain brought a delicious coolness. I played worse even than usual. I was not required for the intermezzo and made my way to the commodities. There I applied the cerussa to my face and neck. Training back to my place, white as a ghost and shaking like an aspen in a gale, I received from Maestro Galuppi a glare and a gesture of dismissal.

Back in the dirt-house, I dispelled the excremental odours with tobacco. The musical piece, which was admirably played and sung, won some applause. I heard the sounds of supper, then of toasts, and then of carriage wheels coming in from the Piazza and leaving again. Little by little, the palace became quiet and, at last, as silent as a churchyard at midnight. Nobody minds the seconds.

In my chats with Mr Edgar and other of the Jack servants, and from the most exact observation of the outside of the palace, I had gained a fair notion of the order and disposition of the several galleries and chambers, and had drawn for myself a wee plan. The King's apartment lay on the west side, on the first level, but my scheme was to pass along the floor above where the Queen had lived. That saintly lady, a Polish princess who had brought King James a great dowry, had died some years before. I jaloused that her rooms would be empty but that there might be some common, or communicating, escalier between the two suites of royal chambers. If there were not, I would hide out in the Queen's apartments till the next night.

All went well enough at first. Taking the dirt-house lantern, I climbed the turnpike stair to the second landing-place, which opened on what had been the chapel, which had since been moved. The floors were of stone or tiles without the carpets of colder climes. Carrying my shoes in one hand, and the bussola in another, I shuffled down the east side, with the apartments of the Princes on my left hand and a courtyard beneath me on my right. The place seemed to consist of several buildings clagged together, for I went up and down for no especial reason. The palace smelled of the smithy, as if the dog-days of two centuries had pitched camp. In the south-west corner, there was indeed a secret or marital staircase and seated before it, with his pistols in his lap, was my friend Mr Edgar.

He stood up and levelled both pieces at my breast. He said: "I have been expecting you, Col. Neilson."

"I am glad. Shall you announce me to His Majesty? As you can see, I am not armed."

He glanced, as so often, at my fiddle-case.

I said: "If you would be so kind, will you guard the instrument during my audience?"

I set the case on the floor. I raised my arms and

said: "You may search my clothes, Mr Edgar, if you wish."

He shook his head. He turned to allow me to pass.

At the foot of the stair, there were two doors. I did not think His Majesty would sleep in a room facing the south where the morning sun would bake him in bed like a breakfast-bapp. I extingued the lantern, put it down and knocked on the western door. There was no answer. I pushed at it. Before the bed, with his back to me, in his night shirt, King James of Scotland, England and Ireland was kneeling at his prie-dieu. He was alone. I stood, upright but uncovered, for an age.

King James rose and, without turning, said in English: "Have you come to kill me, Colonel Neilson?"

"Sire, I bring you something that will gladden your heart and mend your broken fortune."

"Can you bring me Derwentwater in all his pieces? Can you bring me Balmerino and Kilmarnock, and gallant Joseph, vicomte de Durfort? Can you resurrect your brave Irish men blown to pieces by round shot or poignarded in the heather?"

"Sire, I put before you the means to avenge them."

I placed the diamond on a table at his feet. I said: "This jewel was given to me by Major O'Crean at the moment of that good Christian's death. It will equip a force for Scotland without recourse to His Holiness or the Courts of France or Spain. It will build you ships in Riga, Stockholm and Saint-Petersburgh and raise you men in Ireland, Hesse and the Carolinas. I have reason to believe that Her Tsarian Majesty will buy the jewel. You have many friends at that Court. I am certain Her Tsarian Majesty will receive me at Saint-Petersburgh in private interview."

King James looked away from the diamond and searched my face. He had that melancholy, Spanish air that I remembered from the Prince of Wales at Culloden House.

"Will you command my force in Scotland, Colonel Neilson?"

"You have officers more capable than I am, sire."

"It is you that I trust, Colonel Neilson."

I said: "Sire, I will command your armies in Scotland and win back your kingdoms for you, though it cost me everything I hold dear."

"Thank you, Mr Neilson," he said. "You have done me service. I wished to know if there were one true man left on earth. There will be no campaign, not this summer, nor next, nor ever again. We are passing into oblivion." He stood up and held out his hand for me to kiss. "Go back to your fine lady, and put the jewel on a ribbon round her neck and say that James Stuart, that poor marionnette, wished it."

"Sire, may I inquire why?"

"I shall not answer. Present your duty to the Prince of Wales."

I walked out backwards. At the stair-head, Mr Edgar was where I had left him.

I said: "Would you kindly direct me to the apartment of His Royal Highness?"

"His Royal Highness is not in residence."

"Are you sure, Mr Edgar? I am commanded."

He looked at me, turned and set off by the way I had come. By way of conversation, I said: "I am sorry about your men I fought in the Casentino. I hope none came to any great hurt."

Mr Edgar made no reply.

I now saw that the Providence that had preserved me in Venice had shown me the only way to the King. For since the Prince of Wales was in hiding, or at least in *incognito*, there had been no attendants before his apartment, and I had passed unscaithed. Mr Edgar opened a door, handed me my lantern, and stepped back, still holding the fiddle-case.

In the first room, two bravos were asleep before an

empty flask of wine. The next chamber was empty but smelled of grappa and piss. At the far end was a door. I knocked but there was no answer. I pushed on the door which opened on the stench. By the lantern-light, I saw a bed and two persons in a tangle of bed-linen. One was the Prince of Wales, snoring like a sow. The other was a woman, also asleep. Her shift had ridden to show a wide rump marked by scratches. All about were discarded clothes, upended bottles, cold candle stubs and brimming piss-pots. My heart burned for King James, for not all the kingdoms on earth can redeem the loss of a son. I said aloud:

"It had been better, sire, that we had both stayed on that fatal moor."

The Prince stirred but did not wake.

Outside, I said to Mr Edgar: "Come with me into France. My lady designs to carry out a scheme of engineering on her lands in the Sologne and commands me to recruit the good men I can find."

He shook his head. "I shall stay until the end."

"You will take, leastway, my violin."

My treason I take with me.

PART 3

A Dusty Bridegroom

XLIV

At Civita Vecchia, there was a felucca bound for France. We had plain sailing to Leghorn, but a squall caused the captain to stand off Nice, and we landed in the rain at Antibes, where there were letters for me at Bruquier et Cie, rope-chandlers, and a credit of one hundred gold louis from Mme de Maurepas. She must have sent bills of exchange to every port on the coast, Genoa and Barcelona comprised. I bought a fine Neapolitan mare with a high step. There are inconveniencies to loving a woman of property, but also benefits.

The first became more apparent, and the second less so, once I was mounted. The mare and I disagreed as to which way we should go, what pace we should employ and often whether we should go at all. It was a time before we came to an understanding, but by the evening of the first day we were good friends.

Mme la marquise's letter read:

If you have this to hand, it means you have done your business and returned to France for which I offer thanks to God. The gazettes are full of M. Hamilton's escape from under the Leads, but Monsieur B. sent an express with exact information, which is yet more fantastical. There is small-pox at Vierzon, but God has up to this day spared our people, except poor Ballin, who has a little companion in that foolish bourg. You will recollect that he excused himself from the vaccination. My farrier is treating him by the Perso-Scottish system.

In the late promotion, you are to have a brigade and the red ribband. Also, your friend at Rome has written to inquire of me, as one of your principal or favoured concubines, if you will accept from H.M. a thistle. Since I do not know if that is reward or punishment, I could answer him only in general phrases. As for the Scotch Earldom you are to request, my darling and I have been reading Mac-Beth and can find nothing worthy of your merit.

Mr H. is to marry! I have wrote to his bride at

Dorkinge in as affectionate a tone as my wretched English will allow. I said that though our men love to fight one another, we ladies may be friends. I have asked her to visit just as soon as peace is concluded.

A certain person writes to you every day. She piles her letters in a sort of siege-tower on my escritoire and, since she is advancing also in mathematics, numbers them in M. Fibonacci's sequence. You are to read them in the precise order in which they were written. She grows beautiful, God willing, and has laid by the tomahawk and scalping-knife. A second young person has come to visit and inquires after you.

Come soon, dear friend, and send ahead so we may drive out on the road to meet you.

PS: Monsieur B. at Venice offers A. Mantegna Assumption of Our Lady with Saints (I forget which ones) but his price ruins me at this time. Cannot he send the small Tiziane Maddalena for my refusal?

PPS: My darling tells me you are no longer a Protester, for which I thank God and you, unequally.

I saw that the young person could only be Sergei Pavlovich, son of my Russian friend Countess Bielke. I had met him, as a lad of five or six years old, in Persia back in 'Forty. He must have entered French service under orders from his father to call on me. I was sure that Mme de Maurepas would treat him kindly, and write to his parents at Olenskaya Polyana, their lands in the Smolensk country.

Mr Edgar is, like all the Jacks, a man of no tact but there is no harm done. But why, oh why, has my lady written to Miss Belcher? With her head in the clouds, what can Mme de Maurepas know of a self-conceited English bride? My mind's eye heaved with lawns and tea-tables, all ears to Miss Charlotte Elizabeth. "I have had a letter from our Ambassador in Holland, enclosing another from a gentlewoman of France. She is the Marchioness of Maurepas. (They are all marchionesses and duchesses down there.) The lady is allied to Harris' unhappy friend Neilson and wishes mightily to be mine. She passes her mornings writing letters in Swedish about the proper names of plants, while Neilson lolls about her kennels. I understand His Majesty is more inclined than not to pardon him, but Neilson won't ask for it, won't leave his botanical madame. I shall know her, a little, to humour Harris, but I wish at moments that the institute of marriage in France had not so fallen into decay."

My treason ate at my breast. For the sake of Father

O'Crean and my murdered Irish men, I had betrayed not my mistress alone, but also Captain Harris, who had not dragged me off Culloden Moor so that I might take up arms anew against the King his master. I saw that whichever course I took I must betray trust, but Mme de Maurepas and Mr Harris were living and might (after some time and recollection) grant me pardon.

I made no especial haste. I did not wish to disgust my mount with the affair of transportation, and rested her each second day. We passed a farm, which was calling for hands for the vintage, and, for the wage of turning out the mare on autumn grass and an admirable supper, I passed a day among the vines till I was rigid with grape sugar.

We crossed the River Cher at Mennetou. Once in the low country, I gave the mare her head, and wandered through the twilight, smoking my pipe, and wondering: Why is my mistress buying Mr Law's pictures? There is nothing more in this world below than a sorrowful old soldier, without a nation or a sou to his name, bickering with his mistress in the deeps of France.

When we were good and truly lost, I had a mind at last to be a human being. There was a lake on one side (I will not say which side) which pitter-pattered in the rain. I walked my horse down into it up to her elbows. Then with a muttered *"besmellah"*, I threw the diamond as far from me as I could. From a distance, I heard a splash of water.

Yet the thing must have its revenge. Turning the rein, I found the mare could not move. She was becoming agitated. I dismounted, and dived down to dig out each foot, while she thrawed and whined. At last, I had her clear and led her to the bank, but found that in her convulsions she had cast a shoe. There was no remedy but to lead her. We were soaked to the skin. The wind cut like butchers' knives. From a distance, I heard the barking of a dog.

Ahead was a swinging light. A child's voice came down the wind. Before us was a barefoot girl, at her wits' end.

"Sir, sir. Come quickly. Claudine is dying. Come quickly."

We blundered after her to a low steading, out of which came sounds of massacre. I drew sword.

"Please stand behind me, lass. Hold the lantern as high as you can."

Mme Claudine was a Gascon sow, cast in her stall. The den was too small for her and she had become wedged on the narrow side. Her spine was two or three degrees out of true. She was shrieking in pain and rage.

"Bring me your father's axe."

The child sprang at me. "You shall not kill Claudine! She is my pet!"

"I shall not touch your precious Claudine. Bring me the axe."

On tip-taes, she pulled a great hatchet down from the rafters.

"Now, go and water my horse. Quick, lass!"

The stall was walled with upright oak pales, old at the conversion of Clovis the First. They were held by a cross-piece pinned with iron braces. With all my strength, I brought the axe down on the cross-bar. The wood began to splinter, and then burst in a roar. Pales, timbers, stones, plaster, iron and pig rained down upon me. I dusted myself down. Restored to her regular geometry, the monster turned, grumbling, to her scraps. The girl sniffled.

"Now, young lass, you must saddle me your father's horse. He shall keep my mare in fair exchange till I return."

"We have no horse. We have many, many geese and rabbits. And Claudine."

We were not entirely on the same plane of discourse and understanding.

"Please show me the road to La Ferté-Joyeuse."

She pointed up the hill, where a glow was coming into the sky.

"Is it far?"

"Very far, sir."

I reached for my mount's bridle. The girl shifted from bare foot to bare foot. "Sir, if you bide an hour and help capture the geese, there will be carts going over to the fête."

"What fête?"

"Don't you know? Everybody knows. Her Ladyship is to marry—"

"Whom is she marrying? Quick, girl!"

"Stop! You're frightening me."

"Forgive me. Do you know the name of the gentleman Her Ladyship will honour?"

The child sulked. "A great king or prince. For she is beautiful and rich."

I was running, holding onto the stirrup leathers.

Mme de Maurepas has betrayed me as I have betrayed her. That Court in Rome could not keep a secret for five minutes. She knew when we parted that I would offer King James my service. My darling, you and I cannot now fight, but we can try to dissuade her. Come, my darling, just this last stretch and I swear by God that you shall live your life at pasture and run all summer-long with your foals.

We crested another slope and, of a sudden, in the far dawn light, was the castle of La Ferté-Joyeuse. She looked so gallant and gay, the flags unfurled on the towers, the stone and brick just taking colour of white and rose, wreaths of smoke above the kitchen pavilion, the glimmering Sauldre, rides radiating through the park and woods into eternity. Beneath me, the road descended in a succession of curves. Thinking to save distance and time, I resolved to cut the corners, but the slope was too great, my mount lost her footing, and we tumbled downwards through briars. My horse was reluctant to stand.

"It is just us, horse. I will mount now. Do what you can. You can do no more."

XLV

We stagger through the gate and under the lime trees. Through the mist in my eyes, everything is transfigured. The bridge teems with carts and beasts and women. The men of the guard are running out of the guard-house, fumbling their powder-horns, musket-butts rattling on the pavement, the officer's wig aslip. The farrier stands petrified, a flaming horse-shoe in the air. The late duke's silver wine cistern, the size of a horse-bath and blazoned to extinction, bristles with Champagne. An ingot of ice slips from its sling at the cart-tail and smashes to pieces on the pavement. Above the four towers, the banners of St Louis and St Andrew, two-and-two, snap and billow in the fluent air.

On the top step, Mlle Marie-Ange de Joyeuse, in dress, rocks an infant swaddled in white linen. Mme Marrin, also in dress, is laughing like a church gargel. I swoon. The mare goes down on her front knees. I try to roll off but my spurs are caught in the stirrup-irons. Pierre Dalouhe has his fingers in her nostrils and she rises with a groan, falls back, rises again. He is speaking to her but I cannot hear.

The leaves of the door open. From out of darkness, Jeanne de Joyeuse comes to the top of the steps. She blinks in the low sunlight. She is barefoot and a damp patch is spreading from her breast to her shawl. Her cheeks are all healed. There is a splutter of musketry. I hear shouts of "Long live the Brigadier!" And: "Long live the Chevalier Neilson!"

A DUSTY BRIDEGROOM

Jeanne de Joyeuse blinks again and descries her dusty bridegroom. She laughs. She descends the steps, holding up her night-gown, and then, with one foot on the lowest tread, places the other on the ground.

To be continued.